'I think he'd bet[...]
Nurse, just in ca[...]
under supervision[...]
this to the wife, a[...]
same hospital room as her husband, that Joanna
looked up suddenly, into a pair of brilliant blue eyes
that were watching her with extraordinary interest.
The eyes belonged to a tall man in a smart white
shirt and tailored trousers. She left the room to the
patient and his wife, closing the door behind her.
'Can I help you?' she asked.

'I'm Dan Bruce. You must be Dr Bliss.'

Joanna allowed her hand to be shaken briefly.
'How do you do?' She waited for an apology. She
was surprised at finding that her boss wasn't the
plump middle-aged father figure she had expected,
but a very dishy young man with a magnetic gaze
and a superb physique. But her surprise was over-
shadowed by her anger at his non-attendance when
he should have been on duty. With a voice made
even colder because she was trying not to notice his
very real physical attractions, Joanna said, 'It's a
good thing I was in the hotel, doctor. As my name
was not on the rota for tonight, I might have gone
into Constanza—and then our patient might not
have lived.'

The piercing blue eyes seemed to look into her
very soul. 'You're here to take some of the load off
my shoulders, Dr Bliss. Don't ever speak to me in
that tone of voice again!'

Lancashire born, Jenny Ashe read English at Birmingham, returning thence with a BA and RA—the latter being rheumatoid arthritis, which after barrels of various pills, and three operations, led to her becoming almost bionic, with two man-made joints. Married to a junior surgeon in Scotland, who was born in Malaysia, she returned to Liverpool with three Scottish children when her husband went into general practice in 1966. She has written non-stop since then—articles, short stories and radio talks. Her novels just had to be set in a medical environment, which she considers compassionate, fascinating and completely rewarding.

Previous Titles

MISPLACED LOYALTY
SISTER HARRIET'S HEART
DOCTOR RORY'S RETURN

CARIBBEAN TEMPTATION

BY

JENNY ASHE

MILLS & BOON LIMITED
ETON HOUSE   18–24 PARADISE ROAD
RICHMOND   SURREY   TW9 1SR

*First published in Great Britain 1991
by Mills & Boon Limited*

© Jenny Ashe 1991

*Australian copyright 1991
Philippine copyright 1991
This edition 1991*

ISBN 0 263 77177 6

*Set in 10½ on 12 pt Linotron Times
03-9103-48914
Typeset in Great Britain by Centracet, Cambridge
Made and printed in Great Britain*

CHAPTER ONE

OUTLINED against a Caribbean sky of ultramarine silk, the man seemed tall. He was naked from the waist up, and his fair hair was long, curled on to a strong neck. The muscles in his back stood out as he half turned, leaning on his scythe, to look down the grassy bank at the side of the mountain track.

'Constanza? Yes, you're on the right road.' His English was good, but sounded as though it wasn't his native language. And his eyes—as blue as the sky behind him—showed nothing but amused contempt. 'But you'll never make it in that tank. You need a jeep to get through the mountains—or at least a four-wheel-drive.'

Joanna was driving a small Japanese car she had hired at the airport. 'That's hardly my fault. They didn't warn me.'

He shrugged, and said pityingly, 'I suppose if it doesn't rain you might get by. You're new to Hernandez, then?'

'Yes—very new. I've never been out of England before.' She watched his lip—and it curled as she expected, with what she interpreted as condescension. Unpleasant fellow, in spite of his good looks. She turned her attention back to the road. 'Well, thank you.' Her voice was curt as she found first gear and pressed hard on the accelerator. He hadn't offered any constructive advice, only criticism. And

5

that was pointless, because she was already halfway
to Constanza, and there was nothing she could do
about the car now, except pray that it made it up the
winding track and down into the valley before dark.

The road was deeply pitted and rutted by former
hurricane rains. Joanna Bliss was too busy concentrating on her driving to worry too much about why
a blond blue-eyed man was scything grass at the side
of the road, on a Spanish Caribbean island peopled
by mulattos. He was ruggedly handsome. But
Joanna had very definite views on men or women
who were deliberately rude or unhelpful to
strangers. Señor Blond had been unhelpful, to say
the least. Joanna decided she wasn't a bit curious
about what he was doing there.

Inside the rainforest, the path was easier to nego-
tiate, as the sun was hidden, and the dappled glades
were quite magically lovely between massive bam-
boos as thick as oaks, and delicate tall fern trees.
Streams tumbled, glittering in the gleams of sun
between the branches, and deep ravines would seem
impossible to cross, until the road turned a corner
and wound steadily onwards, shored up where the
sides were too steep.

Then suddenly she was out in the sun again, and
the road levelled and started to descend. The peak
of the mountain was past, and now she could see the
sunlit coastal valley across pale grass and scattered
rocks. There was the little town of Constanza, with
its tiny neat fields of pineapples and bananas, its
miniature goats, chickens and geese. And beyond,
spread out along the glittering palm-fringed beaches,

were the elegant thatched villas and tailored golf courses of the Palacio Hotel, her final destination.

She could perhaps understand the blond man's warning—the road down was worse, and she jolted perilously near to the edge at times, very glad that the mud road was dry today, baked by the hot sun. But now that she could see the town, she felt safe, and covered the final few miles with new optimism.

The Palacio was luxury such as Joanna had only seen in films. 'Dr Bliss—a pleasure to welcome you!' Señor Riaz, manager of the hotel, rose from his executive desk to shake her hand warmly. Through the open window behind him she could see the Caribbean, sapphire sprinkled with diamonds, and the smooth green of the golf links edged with palms. Señor Riaz was Spanish, with heavy black eyebrows and dark rings under his eyes, giving him an air of genial dissipation. 'Had a good journey?' he asked.

'Yes, thank you. I hired a car at the airport.'

'You drove alone through the mountains?' He too seemed surprised she had risked it. 'I could have sent someone to meet you.'

'I wanted to see something of the country. It's spectacular.'

Señor Riaz smiled, but seemed to decide to say no more about the risks, as she had arrived safely. 'I'll introduce you to the medical centre and show you your quarters. Then I'll leave you to relax until cocktails. Dr Bruce, your chief, will be joining us before dinner.' He led her along marble-tiled corridors, across floodlit patios and walkways filled with climbing and fragrant plants, where hummingbirds and gaudy macaws flew free.

Joanna's step was light. At her dingy grey hospital in the Midlands of England, the consultants never had time to join them for cocktails before dinner! Perhaps Roger had been right after all—a year away would be good for her, broadening her horizons before she went back to take up a trainee GP job in that same Midlands town, in a practice as grey as the hospital.

Señor Riaz pointed out the five swimming pools, the cocktail bars, tennis courts and outdoor dance-floors, each with its own small orchestra. Joanna said, 'Now I see why you couldn't manage with only one medical officer. All these staff! It must run into hundreds before you even count the guests who might need a doctor.'

Señor Riaz said proudly, 'It is the biggest hotel complex in these islands. Hernandez came late to tourism—long after Jamaica and Bermuda, all the established places. We profited from their experiences, and my company was able to plan what we consider the perfect holiday experience. Hence our name—Palacio. We want our guests to feel they have lived like royalty.'

'Working here will be a pleasure, not like work at all.'

'I hope so, Doctor. The clinic is well planned—as comfortable as our hotel rooms, I think.' He stopped outside a thatched villa, overlooking the golf course. 'And this is yours. I hope you are happy here. There is a maid to see to whatever you need.'

Joanna's eyes were wide. But she managed to conceal her amazement, when she thought back to the cupboard of a room she had lived in at the doctors' residence in Moreton! 'Thank you, Señor Riaz.'

'When you have settled in, the medical centre is just across the gardens to your right. Do prowl around, Doctor, and find your bearings. I shall expect you at the main pool at eight.'

Joanna's suitcases were already unpacked inside the cool bedroom, her clothes hanging up neatly. The villa had cream walls, with Spanish pictures, dark green shutters and a tiled floor. A fan on the ceiling twirled lazily, and at the back of the room a dark-skinned maid, dressed in pale blue, drew back the curtains, bobbed her head politely. '*Señorita*, my name is Rosita.'

'Oh—but. . .' Joanna was embarrassed. If only this young lady knew how humble was Joanna's background, and how she was already overwhelmed by the Palacio, without having a maid to look after her. She decided to be honest. 'Rosita, I've never seen such a place!'

'But *señorita*—you are from England!'

Joanna laughed. 'England isn't all like Buckingham Palace and Kew Gardens. My family aren't well off.'

The maid clearly didn't believe a word. 'You want anything ironed? I pour you a drink? Choose dress for evening?'

Joanna looked ruefully at the line of modest dresses, as Rosita went through them, one by one, in the slatted dark wood wardrobe. How ordinary they seemed, in this exciting, vivid place. The brightly dressed hotel guests made her feel dowdy. Joanna had worked hard at her housemanship, then trained as casualty officer. Clothes hadn't seemed important. All she wanted was to find a suitable GP job, marry Roger and live in an ordinary little house in Moreton.

She looked out of the window, saw the wealthy golfers on the links, suntanned beauties making their way to and from the beach, tall willowy dark tennis pros giving lessons to eager young girls. It was a different world, just for a year. She smiled back at Rosita. 'All these glamorous Americans!' The plump matrons in their false eyelashes and diamonds, the slim tanned girls, the Spanish aristocracy with their glossy hair drawn back from handsome faces, tight dresses, swirling flared hemlines. She rifled through the wardrobe again. Maybe a skirt and top would be better? She had a couple of full skirts that were a little more trendy.

As she tried them on in front of the full-length mirror, Rosita went to the kitchen and came back with a tall glass. 'This is Cuba *libre*—rum and Coke.'

'But I don't like rum.'

'This Hernandean rum. You try.'

Joanna tried, sipped, ice clinking, and sipped again. 'Wow!' she exclaimed.

'Nice, huh?'

'Very nice. But I'd better not drink it all. I'm not used to it.' She put the glass down, feeling slightly more pleased with her reflection now, as the blue skirt flared, emphasising her waist, and the white lace blouse covered up the lack of suntan on her arms and neckline. 'Tell me about Dr Bruce, Rosita, my new boss. How old?'

'Nice man, *señorita*. He was here right from the

start, when hotel quite small. Kind man—very good to all the people.'

So he was oldish, then—probably something like plump, middle-aged Señor Riaz. That was somehow reassuring. A father figure. 'I'd better go along and meet him,' she decided. She twirled around in front of the mirror. 'Not up to Palacio standards, Rosita, but I see there are some boutiques in the hotel—I'll do some major surgery on my wardrobe later!' She was surprised at herself. Already this lovely island had worked some magic on her. Already the small demure Englishwoman was feeling different— worrying about her appearance for the first time, and thinking twice about what to wear.

The medical centre was a log cabin of a place, again with a thatched roof. Inside was yet more unimaginable luxury. The mulatto nurses seemed to have been chosen for their beauty as well as their skill. The girl behind the desk glowed with well-being, her mahogany skin smooth and beautifully made up, the whites of her lovely eyes blue with vitality. Her figure, in its close-fitting blue uniform, was perfection in motion, as she rose and came forward with a smile to take Joanna by the hand and kiss her cheek. 'That is the regular Hernandean greeting, Doctor. You'll find all the women get a kiss on the cheek.'

'Even from men?'

The girl laughed, showing white, even teeth. 'Especially men! My name is Malika.'

'Joanna Bliss.' She was a doctor, yet she felt like a poor relation here, visiting a rich aristocratic family. 'Is Dr Bruce here?'

Malika laughed again. 'Oh, no. He only shows up when it suits him. He is what you call a law unto himself, Doctor. He'll come back when he's on duty, and probably not before.'

Possibly a crotchety old man, then. Joanna didn't care. She was here to do a job, and what delight to have such a well-equipped clinic to do it in. She didn't mind an absentee colleague. 'Who is on duty, Malika?' she asked.

The beautiful receptionist showed her the rota in the plush offices, the cool plant-filled waiting area, the lab, even the small operating theatre, shining with newness and efficiency. Joanna could only stare, thinking of the difference between this and the equipment she had learned her surgery on. She stood for a long time, thinking about the huge gulf between rich and poor, even on Hernandez. 'On my way through the mountains, Malika, I saw people living in caves, and in wooden sheds.'

Malika shrugged. 'Hernandean way of life. But in the Palacio our guests are used to better things, so we must provide them.'

Joanna said nothing. No doubt she would soon get used to Hernandez and its extremes of wealth and poverty. She wandered round her own consulting-room, hardly believing it possible—the leather examination couch curtained in flowery muslin, the handbasin, scented soap, thick towels, all the diagnostic instruments she could possibly need, from stethoscope and sphygmomanometer to speculum and oroscope. Malika said, 'You like it?'

Joanna smiled, lost for words. 'I'd better go and

find Señor Riaz,' she said. It was growing dark, and the whole complex was lit up with coloured lights, floodlights over the pools, candles on the restaurant tables, spotlights on the dance-floors.

Malika pointed the way, across trellised walkways lit by hidden lamps behind cacti and shrubs. The music from the nearest band was catchy, giving Joanna a lift of spirits, making her want to dance in time with the drums. She felt as though she were dreaming, as she walked, her ears enchanted with the music, her skin warm, her eyes ravished by the beauty of her surroundings.

Señor Riaz was sitting in a tree-house enclosure built to overhang one of the swimming pools. Beneath, the pool glittered blue in the lights, and a poolside bar dispensed a galaxy of cocktails. 'Dr Bliss, good evening. You have made yourself comfortable?' He beckoned a dark waiter in a white jacket to provide her with a Cuba *libre*.

'Yes, thank you.' How could she express her total astonishment with this place? She sat beside him and looked across the pool and the subtle lighting in the trees, the pale sea beyond the deserted golf course, and the starlit sky. She added, 'There can't be much illness to care for in such a place.'

'Our guests mainly suffer from the sun, from over-eating or from mosquito bites. But the servants' families are your patients too. Babies get born, children suffer from the usual ailments. You will be kept busy, I promise you, Doctor.'

'I'm looking forward to it.'

Señor Riaz said, 'And if you think of any improvements, you must let me or Dr Bruce know at once.'

'Improvements?' Joanna smiled in the darkness.

Wasn't this paradise? How did one improve on paradise?

Gradually the little enclave filled with other people—administrators, tennis and golfing pros, the men in charge of the shooting range, of the polo stables, of the casino. Joanna was introduced to them and their beautiful Spanish wives, expensively dressed, who made Joanna welcome with the kiss on the cheek Malika had predicted.

But still Dr Bruce hadn't come. Joanna recalled Malika's words—a law unto himself. He certainly didn't mind not being around to meet his new assistant. Señor Riaz said finally, 'I'll take you to dinner, Doctor. We'll try the Jamaica Inn tonight—but naturally, you will eat at any of the restaurants in the hotel at no cost.'

Over Creole chicken, chick peas and fried plantains, by the light of flickering candles, with a guitarist strumming melancholy Spanish love songs in the background, Señor Riaz talked and Joanna listened to the story of Hernandez. It had a long and often bitter history of slavery and misery, of great wealth and total degradation. 'But now, Doctor, we slowly get the balance right. We have a democracy. We have elections. Soon, all Hernandeans will be happy.'

And Joanna wondered what the families who lived in shacks would think of that optimism, from a fat Creole with a cigar in his hand and a large glass of brandy in front of him. But she said nothing. Suddenly Señor Riaz said, 'You are a very beautiful woman, Doctor. I think you come here to get away from a broken love-affair, no?'

She laughed. 'Just the opposite, *señor*. My fiancé suggested it would be good for me to work abroad for a year. He spent six months in India, and he said it broadened his outlook.'

'He is also a doctor?'

'Yes. A specialist in child health.'

Señor Riaz said smoothly, 'He is a brave man to risk sending you to Hernandez. My island has a way of casting spells on people, especially lovely women, so that they find themselves unable to forget her.'

Joanna said, 'He trusts me, *señor*. He knows I will go home after the year is up. We've made lots of plans.'

Señor Riaz smiled, wiped his jowls with a linen napkin, and beckoned for another brandy. 'I'll remind you of your words, Doctor, when your time to return grows near.'

Joanna was ready to point out that she wasn't the sort of person to break her word, in spite of Hernandez's enchantments. But at that moment the head waiter came to their table. '*Lo siento*, Doctor, but the telephone—someone has collapsed, and has been taken to the medical centre. Dr Bruce is not there.'

'I'll go at once.' Again she recalled the receptionist's warning—Dr Bruce seemed to have a very casual attitude to his work. He was supposed to be on call tonight. It was very irritating, on her first day, to find she had an unreliable colleague. It might be Hernandez's way, to take things easily. But Joanna was trained in one of Britain's finest traditions, and the lazy '*mañana*' attitude annoyed her. She hurried along the subtly sensuous walkways, no longer lingering to absorb the atmosphere, but in her mind working out the differential diagnosis of sudden collapse.

Malika was waiting at the clematis-wreathed porch, and looked relieved when she saw Joanna. 'The nurse is with him,' she told her.

'It's a man? How old?' Joanna found her full skirt a nuisance now, and wished she had worn something simpler.

'About sixty.'

She reached for her stethoscope the moment she entered the examination-room. A dark, beautiful nurse was taking the blood-pressure of a stout, red-faced man, whose breathing was rough and loud, and whose flowered holiday shirt looked out of place on a sick man. 'Pressure?' Joanna asked briskly.

'Normal, Doctor.'

She listened to the heart carefully. In a man of this size and age, a cardiac condition was very likely. But there seemed no abnormality in his heart. There were slight crepitations in his lungs. 'Is there anyone with him?'

'They're finding out.'

Joanna held the pulse again. Regular. She hadn't asked about facilities for doing blood tests. 'Has he regained consciousness at all?'

'No, Doctor.'

'Ten-ml syringe, please. I'll take some blood. And will you try for a water specimen?'

The distraught wife could be heard through the open windows, as Joanna found a vein and began to draw off blood for testing. There was a dull pallor under the red of the man's sunburn that made her think of diabetic coma. She released the blood carefully into a testing bottle, while the nurse covered the vein puncture with a small plaster. As the sobbing drew nearer, Joanna went out to speak to the wife. She also was large, wearing a loud black and white flowery dress and carrying a fat white handbag. 'I told him not to go off without his glucose tablets!' A broad Brooklyn accent.

'So he is diabetic—I suspected it.'

'He needs his sugar! It's happened before. I could tell he wasn't well two days ago.'

'Two days ago? In that case, I don't think it's a hypo attack. The collapse would have been more sudden. Would you wait a moment with Nurse?'

The plump woman stared. 'I thought you were the nurse.'

'I'm Dr Bliss. If you don't mind waiting——'

'You're only a kid! Where's the proper doctor?'

Joanna said firmly, 'Please wait. Did your husband take his insulin normally this evening?'

'I wasn't with him! But he's been eating at odd times. Oh, I told him not to——'

'Do you know his usual dose?'

'He has it round his neck—engraved on a metal tag! Are you sure you know what you're doing?' The woman tried to push into the room, but while the nurse and receptionist held her back, Joanna found the tag, which had snapped and slipped down inside the flowery shirt, and discerned the dose of insulin which the patient obviously hadn't taken that evening. She found the drug in the locked, refrigerated supply cupboard, and carefully injected the correct dose.

'Please feed him intravenously until his condition is stable. And he'll need some antibiotics for that chest too.' She set up a drip, and inserted the needle into a vein in his left arm, securing it with plaster.

'He's coming round, Doctor.' The nurse was bending over him as his eyes flickered open.

'I think he'd better stay here a couple of nights, Nurse, just in case. I'd be happier if he was kept under supervision.' And it was as she was explaining this to the wife, and arranging for her to stay in the same hospital room as her husband, that Joanna looked up suddenly, into a pair of brilliant blue eyes that were watching her with extraordinary interest. The eyes belonged to a tall man in a smart white shirt and tailored trousers.

She left the room to the patient and his wife, closing the door behind her. 'Can I help you?' she asked.

He was very handsome, rather aloof. His blond hair curled over a white shirt collar, and his muscular torso was clothed now, not naked as she had seen it earlier that day. 'I'm Dan Bruce. Haven't I seen you before somewhere?' That interesting accent, not Spanish but not English either. The man she had met on the mountain path took a step nearer and held out his hand. 'You must be Dr Bliss.'

Joanna allowed her hand to be shaken briefly. 'How do you do?' She waited for an apology. She was surprised at finding that her boss wasn't the plump middle-aged father figure she had expected, but a very dishy young man with a magnetic gaze and a superb physique. But her surprise was over-shadowed by her anger at his non-attendance when he should have been on duty. With a voice made even colder because she was trying not to notice his very real physical attraction, Joanna said, 'It's a good thing I was in the hotel, Doctor. As my name was not on the rota for tonight, I might have gone into Constanza—and then our patient might not have lived.'

The piercing blue eyes seemed to look into her very soul. 'You're here to take some of the load off my shoulders, Dr Bliss. Don't ever speak to me in that tone of voice again!'

CHAPTER TWO

JOANNA sat in her delightful modern kitchen next morning, drinking the chilled juice of fresh lemons and oranges that Rosita had prepared for her the previous day. The view was breathtaking in the pink and gold of the morning, the horizon misty, with tiny boats coming towards the shore after a night's fishing, and flocks of brightly coloured birds chirping and quarrelling in the tall casuarina trees along the path that led to the golf course.

But all these pleasures paled. Joanna was furious. She had been furious all night, until her weariness had forced her to sleep, and she woke up furious, because her new boss was arrogant and idle, and had spoken to her more rudely than he should have spoken to a criminal. She screwed up the copy of the rota Malika had given her. It said that each morning Dr Bliss would be on duty at the same time as Dr Bruce. Only for the afternoons and evenings was there just one doctor on call. The same time! She would have to work alongside the abominably mannered Dan Bruce every morning for a whole year.

She opened the fridge, and found eggs, bacon, bread and fresh butter. But she slammed the door again without taking anything out. She couldn't eat; her stomach was too churned up with her disappointment and anger. How could any man be so completely insolent to a colleague? A colleague, moreover, who had saved the life of one of his patients. Bruce hadn't even thanked her, never mind apologised for being late on duty. She opened the fridge once more, just for the relief of being able to slam the door again.

It was almost nine-thirty. She had to go to work. It was already an unpleasant thought, although it was only her very first morning. Work with Dr Bruce—what a ghastly idea! Taking the first cotton dress she laid her hand on, Joanna dressed quickly, brushed back her fine light brown hair, and tied it back with a narrow ribbon. Forgetting the heady moment last night when she had made plans to revise her lifestyle, buy some lovely frocks and become as vivid and fashion-conscious as the Hernandeans, she closed the door of her little palace, and plodded in the warm morning sun across the gardens towards the medical centre.

'Dr Bliss—good morning.'

It was Malika, sitting at one of the tiny cafés under a tamarind tree, whose fringed pale green leaves cast dappled shadows on the croissants and coffee in front of her. 'Good morning, Malika. Off duty?'

'Oh, no. I work every morning.'

'But it's after nine-thirty!'

'Come and join me,' smiled the girl. 'Nothing ever happens up there for hours. You'd be sitting doing nothing. Sit in the sun and let me pour you some Hernandean coffee. I take it black, but you might like it *con leche*. It's a bit strong until you get used to it.'

Joanna sat down. Malika's gentle disposition made it difficult to stay angry. There was perhaps more to the Palacio than Dr Dan Bruce. 'Thank you. But shouldn't I go and see last night's patient? If he's well enough, he'll want that drip removed.'

'Oh, he is being cared for.' Malika explained why. 'Dr Bruce likes his nights free, so he has a retired doctor from the village who comes over whenever he's asked. His name is Dr Jamis. He stays in at night when we have patients in the ward. You'll soon meet him.'

'Dr Bruce likes his nights free! And he isn't on duty when he should be!' Joanna tried to keep the sarcasm from her voice, but it wasn't easy. 'When does he like to work, Malika?'

When Malika didn't reply, Joanna looked up from her coffee—to see Dan Bruce standing by their table, his eyes unreadable, wearing a short-sleeved shirt, his hands thrust deep in the pockets of his light grey jeans. 'Right now, Doctor. Maybe you'll come along and start work? You've quite finished your breakfast, I hope. I wouldn't want anything inconvenient—like looking after patients—to get in the way of your pleasures.'

Joanna's face burned with anger, but Malika said cheerfully, 'Good morning, Doctor.'

'Morning, Malika.' For the first time Joanna saw him smile. She looked at the receptionist. Yes, a pretty girl with a winning personality. Even sour, arrogant Dr Bruce had to melt when he spoke to Malika—even though Malika was as late as Joanna was. It wasn't fair! Joanna could take any criticism if it was fair, but Dan Bruce wasn't fair. Malika pushed back her chair, but Dr Bruce said, 'No hurry. You take your time. I only want Dr Bliss. Come along,

Doctor.' And leaving Malika to finish her coffee, he took a hand from his pocket to take hold of Joanna's elbow in order to propel her along towards the medical centre.

He didn't let go as they entered the shady foyer, and greeted the nurses who were sitting in their own room chatting. He led her straight into the doctors' common-room. Then he let her go, and indicated a chair. 'Make yourself comfortable, Dr Bliss.'

She sat down, saying nothing. Her mind was going over the contract she had signed when she did not know that this monster was going to be her chief. Surely there must be some clause whereby she could get out in advance of the twelve months? It was intolerable that he could lord it over her like the very worst sort of consultant. At least there were rules in British hospitals. Here on Hernandez it was obviously every man and woman for himself. He was speaking again, still standing. 'Don't you want to look at me, Doctor?'

Joanna looked up coldly. 'Yes?'

His eyes were very handsome, topped with those pale bushy eyebrows, the mop of white-blond hair showing his tanned skin to advantage. She found herself admiring him instead of resenting him for a moment, and looked away again quickly. He said, 'What were you going to say?' in a deceptively gentle voice.

She replied honestly, 'I was wondering if there was an escape clause in my contract.'

'You want to go home?'

'I don't want to. But I didn't expect to be treated like a servant, Doctor. I don't know what your qualifications are, but I'm not a new houseman ignorant of medicine, and——'

'I could see that last night.'

'See what?'

'That you knew your stuff, Doctor. You handled that diabetic very professionally. And you dealt with the relative with more tact than I would have done.'

Joanna stared, forgetting that she wasn't supposed to be looking at him. 'You were there?'

'I was there. I sent for you. How else could I find out how you work?'

She was silent for a moment. 'Then I—suppose I should apologise for the way I spoke to you.'

'You most certainly should, Dr Bliss.'

'I think I was influenced by what Ma——' She stopped. She had no right to tell Dr Bruce what reputation he had among the nurses.

He was ironic, moving away from her at last, leaning his elbow on the windowsill and looking out through the Venetian blinds. 'You will have been told that I don't always stick to the printed rules, I expect, Doctor. That I'm not always where I say I'll be? Well, let me explain. As you're my deputy, your job is to obey the rules and stick by the printed word. That's why I requested an assistant in the first place. Is that clear?' He didn't wait for a reply. 'I wrote the rules, and I—and only I—can break them.'

Joanna looked across at him, admiring the way the sun caught his hair, but trying not to let that influence her. 'I didn't realise I was coming to work in a one-party state, Dr Bruce. I was told that Hernandez was a democracy.'

A slow smile spread over his face, brightened his eyes, transformed the room. But he banished it quickly, and snapped, 'I'm telling you this so that there won't be any more mistakes in our working relationship.'

'I understand. I do as I'm told and keep quiet.'

'You're a fast learner, Doctor.'

She was appalled at the way he fielded her sarcasm, the way it bounced off him without getting through. Her heart was thumping with the extra adrenalin his rudeness—and his physical beauty—aroused in her. She said, trying to keep her voice steady, 'Well, now that I'm in the picture, maybe I should go back to my own room.'

'And do what? You have no patients. Anyway, you want to know what sort of cases we get here, surely? And the staff clinic? I hold a clinic over in the servants' apartments once a week. They can come here, naturally, in an emergency, but many of them prefer not to mingle with the guests.'

'Will I take turns with that too?'

'Would you like to?'

'Very much.'

'Hmm—interesting. I thought you would have come out here basically to have a holiday. I didn't expect you to ask for extra work.' Scornful again. Downright rude.

Joanna said, 'I want to go into general practice. The more experience I get with children, the happier I'll be.'

'You have anyone waiting for you? A fiancé? A prospective employer? Or have you come here of your own volition?'

'Does it matter?'

'Not really. Usually young women are running
away from something. Or they have this do-gooder
need to help the Third World. I must say I can't
stand that type.'

Joanna's patience burst. 'Of all the supercilious
bastards I've ever heard! You stand there like God,
being bloody rude about just about everyone!
You've probably grown up thinking that your good
looks can excuse any old bad manners. Well, that's
not the way I see it, Dr Bruce. You can be an
Adonis—but real people see only what's underneath. If that's nothing but arrogance and selfish-
ness, then that's what people will see!' She stopped,
only then realising what she had done. Her anger
faded. Her voice was low. 'And now I'd better go
and pack my things. You'll want me out of here by
tonight, I shouldn't wonder.'

'Wait.' He stopped her before she stood up. She
sat quietly, catching her breath, wishing she hadn't
ruined her whole chance of working in this lovely
place. Dan Bruce moved closer, and waited until she
looked up at him. 'Do you really like me, then?'

She swallowed, and said angrily, 'Does it sound
like it?'

'Quite a lot.' His voice was thoughtful. Then it
changed, and became businesslike. 'Well, Doctor,
now that we've cleared the air, let's get down to
work. Malika will have dragged herself to her desk
by now. Let's go over to the staff clinic, and I'll
show you some of the case notes.'

Joanna stood up, her legs feeling shaky with the
remnants of her anger, and also with Dan Bruce's

last words. He had even twisted her comments into a compliment to himself. What an ego! How could she possibly like such a man? She said slowly, looking at him cautiously, 'I suppose you expect me to be grateful because you didn't fire me on the spot?'

'Not a bit.' His face was impassive. 'I expect you to come along and get on with your work. You seem to be a good doctor. You have a bad temper, but no doubt you can live with that. It doesn't bother me.'

He opened the door for her. As she passed him she felt the warmth of his body, smelt the man of him, the muscle and the sweat and the aftershave, the clean cotton of his shirt. And while she waited for him to tell Malika where they would be, she looked out of the open doors into the warm garden of hibiscus bushes and flame trees, and wondered how you could dislike someone so much, and yet still have, suddenly, a kind of fierce attraction to him.

The clinic across the road, where all the hotel workers had their quarters in squat comfortable apartment blocks, was much less grand than the medical centre, but it still beat the standards of many municipal and local authority clinics that Joanna had worked in. Dan Bruce led the way, and she noticed how many of their names he knew, how many he stopped and spoke to about some sick relative, or some problem at work. He introduced her to them all as his partner, and Joanna noticed them look at her with wariness. No doubt they thought this new Englishwoman couldn't measure up to the Dr Bruce they knew and trusted. She quietly resolved to prove otherwise.

They walked back slowly. The animosity, the verbal sparring had gone while he told her some of the patients she would have to keep an eye on, and look out for. She had read the case notes in the clinic. Where he could, Dr Bruce had called on the patients, and let Joanna see the problems for herself. There was the usual mix of patients she would be seeing when she got back to England and her GP job. Some were mentally disturbed, some were old and confused, some were inadequate. 'These are your chronics, Dr Bliss,' he told her. 'They may not even know they need you, but if you take on this clinic then you take on those patients. Do you want time to think it over?'

'I've already told you I'll do it.'

'It means seeing your chronics in addition to the ones who come with everyday problems.'

'I realise that.'

When he smiled this time, it was open, genuine, almost friendly. 'Thank you.' They had returned to the centre, and there was a trickle of minor cases waiting to see them, so they separated to their own consulting-rooms, and finished the morning doling out pills for hangovers and dyspepsia, creams for mosquito bites and sunburn, and tranquillisers to those who found their spouses irritating to live with.

When Joanna finished, she sat at her desk quietly for a while, fingering her ball-point pen, and thinking about her new and very disturbing boss. One thing was startlingly clear: she would never be bored. They had weathered a stormy introduction.

Maybe now the relationship could start to settle down into something approaching normal for medical colleagues. She had worked with many a moody consultant, tetchy over work, over money, over not being able to get away for his golf or to get to his children's sports days at some private school in the leafy suburbs. She had thought herself competent to deal with them. Yet suddenly the man she was working for was frighteningly attractive and most unpredictable.

There was a tap at the door, and the man she was thinking about put his head round the door. 'You're on your own, Dr Bliss. My day off,' he announced.

'That's OK.' It was in the rules this time. 'Have a nice afternoon.'

'Malika has Dr Jamis's telephone number. And he will anaesthetise if necessary. You have done surgery?'

Joanna stared. 'Naturally I've done some. But I haven't got any exams.'

'Can you do an appendix?'

'Oh, yes.'

'You'll do. *Hasta luego*.'

'Goodbye, Dr Bruce,' she said calmly, at the closed door. He was in a hurry to be off, that was for sure. She heard an engine start up. Only some privileged few were allowed to drive on the hotel premises. Clearly Dan Bruce was privileged. She found herself smiling. Maybe it wasn't going to be as bad as she thought.

Malika came in, handing her a small black piece of plastic. 'Your pager, Dr Bliss. The nurse on duty will bleep you if you're needed. Would you like to come to the beach café for lunch?'

'Very much.' She had forgotten she had skipped breakfast out of pique at Dr Bruce's bad manners. Now she felt very hungry indeed. 'Is this where you usually go?'

'Yes—I usually spend most of the day here. Don't forget to bring your swimsuit. They'll give us a towel there.'

'No patients at all?'

'Only emergencies. Usually none. The guests are all out enjoying themselves.' Malika looked at Joanna's white arms. 'The sooner you get yourself a tan the better.'

'Not too fast, though. It's dangerous for fair people.'

'Right. So we'll find a lounger under the trees.'

They ate pizza and salad and drank large glasses of mineral water clinking with ice and yellow with lemon slices. Joanna hesitantly asked Malika about Dr Bruce. 'He rushes off so fast. Has he a family?'

'Not as far as I know.'

'I don't recognise his accent. Is he foreign?'

Malika laughed. 'Foreign to us on Hernandez! He's from Jamaica. You recognise the twang in his English? His family came from Britain, but he was born in Kingston. I think he studied in the States.'

'I wonder where he goes?'

Malika said, 'We don't ask. But as it's so regular we think it has to be a woman.' She pointed to the beach, full of lissom young women. 'Otherwise why wouldn't someone as attractive as he is stay here and have his pick of the talent?'

They swam out to the coral reef, where royal terns perched on the coral that was just under the surface, looking as though they were walking on the water. The sea was warm and turquoise, and the palm trees leaned over the white sand towards the water, just as Joanna had seen in all the tourist brochures, and not believed anywhere could be so picturesque for real.

Some American boys were playing handball quite close, with a line strung between two casuarina trees. They were bronzed and good-looking, and quite naturally soon began to address comments to the two girls, who by that time were almost asleep on their loungers. Eventually they asked Joanna and Malika to referee the match, complaining that one of the teams was cheating. It was all very light-hearted. But when they tired of the game, two of the boys came over, bearing gifts of ice-cold cans of cola. 'I'm Chuck, the ugly one is Pete. We're from Massachusetts. You girls on holiday too?'

Joanna smiled. It wasn't the first time she had been mistaken for a girl ten years younger. Malika was explaining that they worked here, and didn't have too much time off. But the lads were persistent. 'What harm to meet us for a drink tonight? You can teach us the local dances.' It was almost a relief when a sharp tone came from Joanna's pager, start-ling the boys.

'That's our boss,' said Malika. 'We have to go.'

Pete sprang to his feet when the girls stood up, and Joanna smiled at him, impressed by such a display of good manners. On closer acquaintance, he was older than the others, and as Chuck was teasing Malika, Pete said to Joanna, 'It would sure be nice if you could make it.'

'Are you in charge of these boys?'

'I'm the eldest. Final year at agricultural college. I only came to keep my kid brother Paul out of mischief.' They were walking along the beach towards the way out back to the hotel. He was gentle, soft-spoken and good company. Joanna half promised she would venture along to the restaurant the boys had mentioned, and he looked pleased. 'You're real pretty, Joanna. I love the way you folk talk—so ladylike!'

It was only later, after Joanna had dealt with a boy who had trapped his fingers in a door, and the boy's mother, who had fainted at the sight, that the girls managed to speak together. Malika liked Chuck. 'And Pete is cute, isn't he?'

'Cute, very,' Joanna agreed. 'But I didn't tell you—I'm engaged.'

Malika was scornful. 'It's no big deal, Doctor.'

'Call me Joanna, please.'

'You're not eloping with the boy—only helping him have a nice holiday. A few drinks, a dance or two—hell, Joanna, if you don't loosen up a little, you'll never fit in here. It's Hernandez, man. No problem!'

'All right.'

'What's the matter? You've gone quiet.'

They were sitting in the waiting area of the centre, surrounded by potted palms and listening to the tinkling of the miniature fountain in the corner. Joanna felt she knew Malika well enough by now to confide some of her thoughts. 'It's Roger,' she explained. 'Do you know, I feel quite guilty?'

'For refereeing a handball match with some high-school kids?'

'No, not that. It's just that—I haven't even thought of him. I haven't missed him. I can't even remember what he looks like properly. It's as though I only met him once, a long time ago.'

The other girl looked knowing. 'It figures, Joanna. After all, ever since you arrived you've been busy living a whole different life, getting to know your way around. Getting to know our mutual big chief Dr Bruce. Now that's a handful for a start!'

Joanna looked guilty. 'You heard me shouting at him?'

'I think everyone heard you,' grinned Malika. 'He deserved it. He throws his weight around if no one stands up to him.'

'Why do you let him?'

'Because we all love him, I guess. Best-looking boss in the hotel—and that's counting all the tennis pros, as well as Valentino himself from the polo stables.'

'So what I told him was right. He gets away with bad manners because of his looks.'

'Right. It's a good job you're engaged, Joanna, or you might fall for him too. And then we'd have no one to stand up to him.'

Joanna took a deep breath. Life was interesting, suddenly. And puzzling. Why couldn't she visualise Roger's face in her mind? Why hadn't she even thought of him last night? She had almost made a date with a stranger she had run into on the beach.

And even now she kept looking over to the car park under the trees, restless to see her difficult and impossible chief come back. Yet she knew very well that he never came back when he was off duty.

Joanna made a sudden decision. 'You're right—it won't do any harm to go dancing tonight. But I've nothing to wear. Come to the shops with me, Malika, and help me buy something really fun!'

'Sure! That's what the Palacio is all about. Let's go.' But even while she cheered Joanna on, Malika was efficient enough to re-set the pager and put it in Joanna's shoulderbag, reminding her not to change bags without changing the contents. When Joanna commented, she smiled. 'I've been here a long time. We believe in an easy time—but Dr Bruce would never trust me again if a single patient suffered because I'd forgotten to do my job. He likes his time off. But when he's on, Joanna, there's no one cares more about his patients.'

'You really do love him, don't you?' teased Joanna.

'In my own way, yes. I told you, all the nurses do.' Malika's smile was broad and infectious. 'But for my real passion. . .' She paused and looked as though she was going to tell, but then laughed again. 'It's my secret!'

'Then I won't pry.'

'But not many miles away from the polo fields! Do you like polo, Joanna?'

'A bit out of my league, I'm afraid.'

'Not here. Everyone rides, you see. Everyone is at home on a horse. It's just that no one looks quite as gorgeous as Valentino.'

And Joanna was smiling to herself at the obvious adoration in Malika's voice when the girl said, 'And he's got this super friend, Fidel. I think you'd get on well with Fidel, Joanna.'

The grey, indistinct face of her fiancé hovered, and Joanna hastily changed the subject. It was almost as though Hernandez itself was conspiring to take her mind from the man she loved, and she had no intention of that happening.

CHAPTER THREE

MUCH later that evening, when Joanna had danced in her new red dress until her feet ached, she sat in a quiet corner of the restaurant and talked to Pete. 'You didn't tell me what it is you do around here,' he remarked.

'Nothing much.' She didn't want to talk about herself. It was nice, being anonymous, being a good listener to Pete, who had many brothers and sisters, and many anecdotes about them that brought his quiet agricultural community to life. 'Go on about Thanksgiving—we don't have that. It's as important as Christmas, then?'

And then the bleep sounded, piercing in the quiet of the restaurant, with only background music and the soft murmur of voices. Pete said, with a rueful smile, 'That sounds to me like a doctor's call. Why didn't I cotton on the first time?'

Joanna nodded. 'Sorry, but I must go. Thank you for the evening.'

He rose as she left the table. 'Here's to the next time, Doc.' He held out his hand, and she gave him hers. He looked into her eyes, holding her firmly so that she couldn't move away. 'I mean it. I haven't enjoyed a night like this for a long time, Joanna.'

When she reached the centre, out of breath, there appeared to be no patient waiting. She pushed open the door, going from the warm night air to the cool of the air-conditioned waiting area. It was hushed and shadowy, with only dim lights on at nearly midnight. Malika's desk, however, was occupied— by Dan Bruce. He didn't get up when she came in. She said, 'Did you bleep me?'

He nodded, and a lock of fair hair fell over one eye. He looked very weary. 'I've had a telephone call from one of the chronics. I'm too tired to see to it.'

'Sure. No problem, I'm on call. Which one? You want me to go to the apartment?'

'No. I've asked the son to bring her.'

'Right. Want to tell me in advance? Or are you checking on my technique again?' she asked.

He smiled wearily. 'Nothing to tell. She's very old. Left ventricular failure and congestive cardiac disease. She has all the drugs she needs for those. Just examine and see why she feels bad. At eighty-four, it might just be *anno domini*.'

'Very well. Why don't you go off to bed, Doctor? I'll manage.'

'She only speaks Spanish.'

'The son can translate. Anyway, I speak some Spanish. Not with a Hernandean accent, I admit.'

He said, 'Who was the clean-cut college boy you were with?'

Joanna stood up straight and stared at him, her chin aggressively lifted. Had he really taken the trouble to look for her? 'It isn't your business,' she said briefly.

'Probably not.' He leaned back in the swivel chair and looked up at her with tired eyes. 'He's smitten, Dr Bliss—couldn't you tell? I hope you're not toying with him.' And in spite of his sleepiness, he smiled rather mischievously.

'I only met——' But the patient was brought in then, pushed in an old-fashioned wheelchair. She was old and wizened, and her chest was wheezing. With a glance at Dr Bruce, Joanna beckoned the son to push the chair into her own consulting-room. While she helped the woman undo the buttons of her dress so that she could listen to her chest, Joanna was wondering how long Dan Bruce had been watching her with Pete Marshall. It was disconcerting.

The old lady was suffering from a patch of pneumonia on one lung base. Joanna gave her an injection of antibiotics, and put her to sleep in the ward with raised pillows, with instructions to take her pulse every hour, and check her breathing.

Dr Bruce appeared to be asleep when she went back to the foyer, leaning back in the chair, his head at an acute angle. She didn't want to leave him there when he ought to be in bed, so she touched him gently on the shoulder. 'Doctor? Hadn't you better get back to your own place? Everything's under control here.'

He opened his eyes, and she thought again how blue they were, the exact colour of a midday Caribbean sky. 'Walk over with me?'

'There's no need. Every doctor I know can walk anywhere with his eyes closed from exhaustion. It comes with the training.' She didn't admit it to herself, but she imagined his tiredness was due to being with his lady friend, and, as such, didn't deserve sympathy.

'All the same, you wouldn't want me to be laid up

with a sprained ankle, just for lack of a friendly shoulder to lean on?'

'No, I definitely wouldn't want that. I'd have to do all your work.' She lent him a shoulder, and they crossed the gardens, towards the main hotel block. 'You live in the hotel itself?'

'I just have a couple of rooms. I'm not here all that much.'

'You have a house in the town?'

'A sort of house, yes.' She walked with him to the lift. He said, 'Can I offer you a drink after your hard work?'

'No, thank you.'

'What is it? Prefer college boys?'

Annoyed, she said, 'I don't "prefer" anyone. I met Pete this afternoon, and we danced, that's all. I'm engaged to be married, and I don't have any interest in other men.'

Dr Bruce put his hand to his head. Was he really as tired as all that? The lift arrived, and Joanna went into it with him, to make sure he was all right. He still appeared dizzy when they reached the third floor, so she walked along the corridor to his door, his arm now about her shoulders, hers round his waist. His body was hard and warm, and she tried not to feel pleasure at touching it. As he fumbled for his key, she said, 'I really don't think there's anything wrong with you. I'll leave you to get to bed.'

But she waited, just to make sure. And once he was inside, it seemed churlish just to go away, when he stood there, his hair falling into his eyes. He might be ill. It happened, even to ill-mannered doctors. 'I'll just warm some milk for you. Do you think you might have a temperature?'

'No. Be all right after a sleep.' And indeed, when he sat down on the sofa, he seemed brighter. He took the milk she had warmed, and a paracetamol. 'Are you really engaged, Dr Bliss?' he murmured.

'Yes.'

'You don't wear a ring.'

'We didn't get around to buying one.'

Dr Bruce put his cup down. 'Know what? The man's a fool to let you out of his sight. If he wanted you to see the world, he should have come with you. He should have married you and gone round the world for a honeymoon. It doesn't make sense for a man in love to send his fiancée to the most romantic island in the Caribbean.'

'Romantic? Is it?' Joanna was watching him closely, humouring him, still unsure how weak he was. 'I hadn't noticed.'

'You've only been here two days. Do you think he doesn't really love you? Is that why he sent you?'

'He's very fond of me,' she snapped. 'He's just—very liberal. Not one of those dreadful male chauvinists.' She gave him a cool stare. 'He believes in absolute equality of the sexes. He went to India last year, so now it's my turn. Anyway, he daren't leave his job to come with me. He's in line for a consultancy. He can't lose his place in the chain of promotion, or he may never get another chance.'

'Sounds a sensible chap.' She still couldn't tell if her chief was mocking her. His tone was neutral, but she felt he was being condescending about Roger. 'Both feet on the ground and all that.'

'That's true,' she agreed.

'And you, Doctor? Are you in love with him?'

'It's an impertinent question. But why else would I promise to marry him?' She stood up. 'And now, as you seem quite well and able to put yourself to bed, I'll get along home. It's nearly one, and my boss tends to make a fuss if I'm late in the morning.'

He stood up suddenly, and, before she knew what was happening, he had put his arms around her and pulled her very close, and found her lips with his. There was very little wrong with the strength in his arms at that moment, and, after an initial struggle, she relaxed and waited for him to let her go. When he drew away, he said, 'That's just to say thank you, and to illustrate what I said about Hernandez. Goodnight, Dr Bliss—have breakfast with me in the morning?'

Joanna walked quickly towards the door, pausing only to say, 'That's just what I might have expected from you. You take what you want, whether it belongs to you or not—time, kisses, anything. You're a very selfish man, Dr Bruce.'

'Will you call me Dan?'

'No. Goodnight, Doctor.'

He watched her go. She didn't look back, aware of his gaze, and only anxious to put the door between them. But as she walked down the stairs, not bothering to call the lift, she put her fingers to her mouth, very conscious of the gentle expertise of his kiss, and of the way his nearness had wrought a great change in the rate of her heartbeat, and the steadiness of her breathing. She was glad she had found the words to tell him how impertinently he had behaved. But somehow, as she turned the key in her own dark green door, she found herself looking back into the shadowy hotel complex, the hidden lights and tall whispering trees, the warm salt air across the golf course, and thinking that he had been right—Hernandez perhaps had more than its share of romance and beauty.

Malika was there at breakfast. Joanna was tempted to try a *tortilla* with her coffee. 'But we mustn't be late today,' she said.

Malika wasn't impressed. 'He isn't like that at all. He usually sleeps until ten. I think he was teasing— trying to give you the wrong idea about himself.'

'There's no need for that. I make my own mind up about people.'

'Sure.' Malika smiled knowingly. 'But when some-one is as fantastic-looking as Dr Bruce, you could be persuaded he isn't as bad as you thought at first.' She was looking behind Joanna's shoulder, towards the hotel. Suddenly she said, 'That's him coming now. In a hurry, it looks like.'

Joanna couldn't help turning. Dan Bruce was indeed coming towards them, and he was striding out as though something was important. As he neared their table, he didn't slow down. 'Good morning, ladies. Something has come up. I'll be back when I can.' And before they could answer, he was nearing his car, taking the keys from his pocket. Joanna watched him. It must be his woman friend again. She watched the long American Ford back out from under the tree, and felt a sense of relief that he wouldn't be breathing down her neck during the morning clinic, as well as an unexpectedly acute sense of disappointment, because, in spite of herself, she had been looking forward to their breakfast together, as he had asked.

Malika said as Joanna started work, 'Maybe he'll come back and do the afternoon for you.'

'He'd better. He should be on duty. I was hoping to go down and explore Constanza today—see the market and the shops, and the natural beach, not the tourist one.'

'You still can. The bleep has a range of over two miles. I'll give you a list of the shops you mustn't miss.'

'What are you doing today?' Joanna asked her.

'This afternoon I'm going to watch the polo. I love the horses.'

'The horses or the trainer?' It was the trainer they called Valentino, because of his dark, brooding good looks.

'I'm not telling,' smiled Malika. 'Come to the match later, if it's still on.'

'I might.'

But when the morning session came to an end, Pete Marshall was standing outside in the midday sun, waiting to catch Joanna as she left. 'Can I buy you lunch?' he offered.

'I get lunch free, Pete.'

'Have it with me?'

'OK. Why not?' They had been interrupted last night in the middle of their conversation. 'But I think I'm still on call. My chief has disappeared from the face of the earth at the moment, so I daren't leave the bleep unattended.'

'My brother has disappeared too,' said Pete. 'I

guess they've all gone into town to get away from me. Paul calls me a drag. What it is to be considered too old to have fun at the age of twenty-five!'

'I was thinking of going to town too,' said Joanna.

'We'll walk down together.' And as they passed the peasants' fields, Pete proved to have a fascinating insight into the agriculture of the Third World. 'The soil here is fertile. They could grow much more than they do, if only they could find the markets.'

They were passing a plantation of bananas, and black women with baskets on their heads were pulling the green hands of unripe fruit, and carrying them to an ancient lorry. 'See that?' Pete paused to watch. 'I'll bet they don't go farther than the next town. It's not the farmers that are at fault—it's the planners.'

'They do well out of sugar, don't they?'

'Very well. But the demand is dropping. That's why you can see all these fields planted with experimental crops. The land around Constanza belongs to the government agricultural research guys. They've realised they can't live on sugar alone.'

'So they're trying to help themselves.'

'Sure. Good luck to them.' Pete smiled at her. 'I must be boring you.'

She assured him she wanted to hear as much as he could tell her about Hernandez. It was more interesting, she told herself, than being informed that it was the most romantic of the islands. But then Dan had followed up his information by a practical demonstration. . . She wondered if he would ever try to kiss her again.

In the main dusty street of the town, they saw

Chuck, Paul and three other boys, kicking around with a football against a group of Hernandeans. It wasn't a busy street, and they could hear the rusty old trucks and motorbikes coming, in time to get out of the way. Pete and Joanna walked past, calling encouragement to the Hernandean side, to taunts from the American boys. The sun was hot, and when they came to a small bar, advertising Hernandean rum, Pete led the way in, and ordered two Cuba *libres* with lots of ice.

They heard women's screams before the screech of brakes. Then there was a hideous scraping of metal on stone. Joanna was out of her seat before Pete realised what was happening, but he followed her into the street, to find an ancient lorry had skidded into a wall. The boys were cowering, white-faced, all eyes staring under the lorry. Joanna ran forwards. 'Someone hurt?' she asked urgently.

'Paul. Underneath. . . .'

Joanna was on her knees at once. She could see the unconscious boy, but not reach him. She crawled out to speak to the driver, who was standing immovable, his eyes terrified. 'Can you drive very slowly forward? Keep the wheel straight. Just a few feet forward?' Her Spanish was adequate for him to understand. She beckoned two of the boys to guide him while she knelt again to see to the injured boy.

The stink of the exhaust was sickening, straight into her face, but she had to see if the boy was all right. The lorry scraped noisily against the wall, one, two, three feet, and at last Joanna could reach far enough to examine the boy's limbs, to test his reflexes, look into his eyes, and make sure he was fit

to be moved. 'His back is OK. But there's a broken
ankle, and a lot of bruising to one side of his face.
I'll need a skull X-ray as soon as we can get him
back.'

She looked up into Pete's tragic face. 'He'll be
OK. But we need transport. Get someone to phone
the hotel hospital for one of their ambulances. Tell
them Dr Bliss needs it. And that I'll need an
anaesthetist! Dr Bruce should be on duty. He can
operate.'

While she waited, she turned Paul very gently into
the recovery position. He moaned and opened his
eyes, vomited a little, then his head fell back loosely.
Joanna comforted him, speaking quietly and firmly,
reassuring him that help was on its way. She had
never set a broken ankle, but she had seen it done,
and was confident she could do it. Paul murmured
something, and she bent down so that her ear was
close to his lips. 'Not his fault. Tell him. Not his
fault.'

Joanna looked up, to where the driver, a small
brown man in baseball cap and overalls, leaned
against the wall, his eyes miserable. She beckoned.
When he came, nervously taking off his cap, she
took his hand, and told him what Paul had said.
'You better go and get yourself a cup of coffee. He'll
be all right.'

The man nodded, obviously still numb with the
shock. She saw him, through the corner of her eye,
slink away round the corner like a wounded animal.
The ambulance came careering along the street,
raising clouds of dust, its siren wailing and scattering
frightened dogs and chickens. Joanna and Pete got

inside with the staff as they skilfully lifted Paul on to the stretcher, and slid it into place.

Dr Jamis was white-haired and shrunken with age. But his eyes were still keen, and he was ready with the theatre nurses to receive the patient. Dr Bruce was nowhere to be found. They cleaned up Paul's wounds, attended to the grazes on his face, and brought the mobile X-ray to check that there wasn't a hairline fracture of his skull. Joanna was scrubbing up, and they brought the X-rays to show her. 'No skull fracture, just bruises, thank God.' Paul was wheeled into theatre, where Dr Jamis gently injected Pentothal, talking quietly until Paul drifted off to sleep. Then he deftly intubated, switched on the halothane, and nodded to Joanna that the patient was ready.

She was calm. She knew she was capable of the operation. But she ought not to have to do it. Dan Bruce should have been here! The ankle had been washed clean of blood, and drenched in antiseptic. She examined it once more, then checked the leg X-rays, to make absolutely sure that she made the incision in the right place. 'No football for you for a month or two,' she murmured, as she retracted the skin and the fascia, and exposed the cracked and splintered malleolus.

'Need any help?'

She looked across. Dan Bruce was gowned and masked. It would have been easy to insult him, but counter-productive. 'I've never actually done this, but I know what to do,' she told him. 'Will you observe, and advise if necessary?'

'Sure. Shall I take those retractors, Nurse?' He

took a position opposite to Joanna. She knew that useless splinters ought to be removed, but that some of the damaged bone would regrow when it was immobilised in plaster. It was a matter of judgement what to remove. Her forceps probed, removed, probed again. Only once she looked up at Dan Bruce while holding a sliver of the tibia. He nodded, and she replaced it in position, and set the repaired malleolus in place before stitching the fascia and skin over it. Dan nodded again, and left the operating theatre. Joanna went with the patient to the recovery-room, and waited until he had regained consciousness before she left to get out of her theatre clothes. Dr Bruce was dressed, his hair neatly combed. She didn't say anything, just got on with discarding her gloves and mask, then went into a curtained cubicle to dress.

When she came out, Dr Bruce had gone. Not a word of apology. Typical. Sister said, 'He went to his room, Doctor. I think another patient came in.'

Joanna didn't go and see him. Why should she? There would only be another row. She just handed the pager to Malika. 'See he gets it,' she instructed.

'Sure.'

'I'll just have a word with Pete Marshall.' Pete was sitting outside the ward, his head down, his shoulders drooping. Joanna went up to him. 'He'll be fine, Pete,' she told him. 'In a day or two we'll fit him out with crutches.'

Pete looked up. 'I was supposed to go along to look out for this sort of thing,' he muttered.

'Here, none of that! It wasn't anyone's fault. OK, the street was a crazy place to play when there is so much open land and beach. There's a saying, Pete—"am I my brother's keeper?" The answer is no.'

She put her hand on his shoulder. Suddenly he stood up and hugged her hard. 'If you hadn't been there——'

'Well, by good luck we were, and it's over.'

He managed a smile through his tears. 'Oh, yeah—all I have to do now is phone the folks and tell them what happened to their little baby boy.'

She rallied him, 'Well, that's one thing I can't do for you, man!'

He took her hand. 'I'll never forget what you did today,' he said fervently.

'Sure.' She watched him walk from the hospital, pause for a word with Malika. And she knew it was a word of praise for her own efforts. She went to the common-room, in search of a comforting cup of tea. It was satisfying to have helped. It was fortunate there was no head injury. Dr Jamis came in then, with more words of praise, and the maid brought them both tea and banana cake, as they discussed the operation, and the old man reminisced about the old days, when they didn't always have halothane in stock.

He left, eventually, after congratulating her again, and Joanna sat for a while in a satisfied lethargy. It was only as she realised it was getting dark that she bestirred herself and stood up. It was evening, and for once, at last, Dan Bruce was at his post, and she wasn't on duty. She could wear another of her new dresses, and take herself to the Jamaica Inn for dinner.

Rosita was there when she got back to the villa.

Rosita always came about mid-morning, cleaned the house and any dishes, and prepared fresh fruit juice. She washed and ironed, then asked if there was any shopping to do. Joanna was still not used to having everything done for her, so she would ask Rosita to make some coffee, and sit and talk to her about Hernandez. Tonight, Rosita had stayed longer than usual, in order to heap praise on her. 'You are so brave, *señorita*. When I first see you, I think you are too small to do the operation. Now everybody talking about you!'

It took some persuasion to get Rosita to go home. At last she went, after making Joanna allow her to run the bath for her, and lay out her new floral dress. At last she could relax in warm scented water, wash her hair, and brush it dry. She sat for a moment and thought about Roger. She ought to write to him. She had been here three days, and did not even want to tell him how she was getting on. She reached out a hand towards the drawer where she kept her writing things.

Then the doorbell rang. She opened the door, half expecting it to be Pete, but it was Dan Bruce. He stood for a moment, and tonight she saw no arrogance in him. He was waiting for an invitation before he even set foot across the door. She said, 'I was just going out.'

'Maybe I could walk with you?'

'All right.'

They began to walk. Across the garden, along the walkways, among the hibiscus hedges and under the frangipani trees that smelled of paradise. 'Why don't you shout at me, Joanna?' he asked quietly.

'What's the point?' He had used her name—without permission. Typical again.

'At least ask me where I was?'

'That's your business.' She was being very cool and professional.

'It is, I know. Private. You wouldn't understand. And anyway, you're paid to do what you did this afternoon.'

She looked at him, and somehow they stopped walking and stood beside the corner of the Jamaica Inn's wooden walls. The guitarist was playing inside—a haunting melody that hung on the air like honey. Joanna said, 'I hear from everyone I meet what a good doctor you are. But I can't say that, because so far I haven't had the chance of seeing you work. All I can tell anyone about you is that you're unreliable, and I won't say that about a colleague. I just have to go on living with it.'

He quietly changed the subject. 'Are you meeting anyone?'

'No.'

'Do you mind if I eat with you?'

There was something in his manner, not to mention his wonderful eyes, hooded now by a worried frown, that weakened Joanna's resolve to stay cool with him. 'No, of course I don't mind. You'll tell me it's in my contract, I expect.'

'I have the impression, Joanna, that you wouldn't do anything you don't really want to. I still think you like me a little, in spite of what you say.'

Like? The word was far too weak. The man was dynamite to be near—one moment blazingly rude, the next being gentle and appealing, bringing out the maternal instincts in her. They were walking now towards the entrance to the restaurant. Joanna contented herself by saying, as he opened the door for her, 'It's nice of you to make sure I never have the chance of getting bored.'

'I'll take that as a "yes", then, shall I?'

CHAPTER FOUR

JOANNA found later that although Dan Bruce had talked quite freely about himself over their quiet dinner at the Jamaica Inn she knew very little more about him. He spoke about his life as an only child of rich colonial parents, living in an opulent mansion on a sugar plantation. He had stories about his life at medical school in the States, and later in Toronto. 'Funny, though,' he mused. 'My folks came from England, yet I've never been there. Too busy, I guess.'

'And now you're Hernandean.'

'Yes.' There was a curtain across his present life, and Joanna was too tactful to try and breach it. 'How about you, Joanna?'

'I'm British, and I intend to go back to Moreton as a GP trainee.'

'You have a job to go to?'

'No. But Roger is looking out for me in all the journals. I've left my CV with him, and I'll start applying after I've been here six months.'

'And you'll marry Roger and live happily ever after.'

'That's the idea.' But it didn't seem quite as attractive as it had only a few days ago. To live in a grey little house in Moreton, send the children to the nearest private school, worry about their exams, visit other doctors' families. . . And always grey

skies, winter woollies, fur boots and constant upper
respiratory tract infections. Here there was hot sun,
clear skies, warm seas—Hernandez was starting to
weave her spell. Joanna had been warned. She
reckoned she had enough strength of purpose to
fight off any false sorcery of tropical paradises.

And so Dan Bruce walked back to the villa with
her. She didn't invite him in, but he went in anyway,
and closed the door behind him. She knew he was
going to kiss her, and she knew she ought not to
allow it, as an engaged woman. Perhaps if she had
been nearer to Moreton her conscience would have
been even more active. But this was a mere holiday,
a passing phase in her life, and, as such, no threat to
her permanent happiness with Dr Roger Fordham.

He followed her to the kitchen. 'Here, let me
show you how to make the perfect Cuba *libre*. It's
all in the lime—not too much, but not too little.'

'Rosita used lemons.'

'Ah, then you haven't had the real thing.' He
opened the ice-box, acting as confidently as though
he lived there in the villa himself. 'You sit down by
the pool, and I'll bring them out.' There was a small
pool in the back garden, subtly lit, surrounded by
reeds and shrubs. Joanna stood, leaning on a low
pedestal, gazing down into the blue water, trying not
to think of Moreton and the grubby little back-to-
back houses where her patients-to-be would live.

She didn't hear him approach. She was turned and
taken into his arms almost before she realised it.
'You're incredibly beautiful, you know that?' She
knew she wasn't, but it was easy to believe it out
here, in a sort of dream world of flowers and birds

and oceans. 'And don't tell me I'm acting without permission. I read the permission in your eyes, Joanna. I don't listen to words when I can see real messages in your eyes.'

She managed to turn her head, so that his searching mouth found only an ear. 'It's a clever line, Dr Bruce. But if I were you I'd save it for someone who enjoys that sort of thing.'

'Who would you suggest?' he whispered, not letting her go.

'About a million attractive women who stay at this hotel.'

'You're very select, then? The only woman who can resist me?'

'Someone has to, or you'll get big-headed.' Joanna leaned away from him, though his arms still surrounded her waist. 'I thought you were mixing drinks?'

'I did. Over there.' And he pretended to loosen his grip just long enough to get a better hold on her, his hand behind her head, his fingers meshed in her hair, so that her lips were imprisoned in his and she couldn't move away. It was sweet and overpowering. This time he wasn't content with one kiss, but stood, his body pressed against her, her back against the marble pedestal, until her resistance crumbled, and she reached up and put her arms around his neck, her hand on his marvellous hair, co-operating in the sensuous sharing of mutual repressed passion.

It was Dan who drew away. Joanna's senses were reeling, and so was her sense of responsibility. It was as though no one had ever kissed her before, so new and vividly exciting was the feel of his skin, his lips and his warm mouth. 'Joanna, my dear, I——'

She came to then, realised what she had been doing, and had been happy to do. She broke away from him and walked down into the garden, giving her breathing time to return to normal. After a while she turned. He had gone. The garden was empty. She heard the gentle click as he closed the front door behind him.

She stayed awake that night, thinking hard. Was her eager response only physical, a natural response to someone who understood what makes women tick? Was it because she was missing Roger? She couldn't remember feeling so intense in Roger's arms, maybe because his physical needs seemed a lot less important to him than to Dan. And did she want to break her engagement? Lose all the hopes and dreams she had nourished since she first entered medical school? Her common sense told her that would be foolish and wrong. Dan Bruce was a stranger—a handsome stranger, who probably had another woman himself, a fiancée, perhaps. This sudden spark between them was only a spark, that died away into the night. With Roger she had a permanent flame, that burned bright and true and would be with her for the rest of her life.

Joanna took breakfast in her own house next morning. It was safer. She had to keep her integrity, her promise to Roger. And the only way to do it safely was not to encounter Dan Bruce in any but the most businesslike of situations. At precisely nine twenty-three, she set off for the medical centre, and sat demurely in the doctors' room, waiting for patients who didn't come, and never had been known to come before ten-thirty at the earliest.

Dan came at nine forty-five. She looked up from the Spanish language newspaper she had been trying to read. What did one say to a man one had passionately kissed the previous night? Dan solved the problem. 'Today you should be over at the staff clinic,' he told her.

She met his look, disturbed by the intensity in the blue eyes, but aware of the need to ignore it. 'You didn't tell me.'

'I'm telling you now.'

She looked away, and folded the newspaper with extra care. 'Very well, I'll go over, then.'

'Thanks.'

Joanna walked across to the staff flats. The clinic was held in a communal room on the ground floor, and a couple of mothers with children were already waiting. She explained in reasonable Spanish that she was the new doctor, and she would be coming every week because Dr Bruce was very busy and had no time. At first the women were doubtful. But their children's coughs, and in one case shrill crying because of an ear infection, made them change their minds. By the end of the morning, news of her kindness and skill had spread, and the waiting-room was full.

She was looking forward to confiding in Dan, to letting him know that the local people had accepted her. But when she got back to the medical centre he scarcely had time to speak to her. 'All OK over there?' he asked.

'Yes, I got on well. No problems.'

He grinned suddenly. 'No problem! That's the Hernandean motto. You're getting acclimatised, Joanna.' Then he picked up a small black medical bag from behind Malika's desk and said briefly, 'Well, I must dash. I hope you have a quiet after-noon at the beach.'

'You're going already?'

'Afraid so. Duty calls.' And he swept out through the glass swing doors like a blond hurricane. Joanna turned to Malika, and they both shrugged.

'Why does he never tell you where he is?' Joanna asked.

Malika said tactfully, 'It must be something per-sonal. We all think he's in love. No one would be in such a hurry to get away if it were just go to the dentist.'

Joanna felt herself blushing, and turned away casually. She had some slight idea what it must be like to be loved by the irresistible Dr Bruce, and was appalled to find herself envying the unknown woman. 'How long has he done this? Rushed away from work?' she asked.

'Ever since I've been here.' Malika tidied her desk and locked the drawer. 'Well? Shall we swim? Or shall I show you round the grounds?'

'Both,' said Joanna eagerly. 'I need a swim to cool off. We can take a walk later. I don't want to sunbathe again—my skin is beginning to burn.'

'OK. We'll buy you a shady hat and stroll round the golf course. Do you play golf?'

'No.'

'If you want some lessons, Mario is very good.

Mind you, he's popular with the guests. But I'm sure he can fit you in.'

Joanna laughed. 'No thanks. It sounds too much like hard work! Anyway, I might get called in the middle of a lesson.'

'That's as good an excuse for idleness as I can think of,' teased Malika.

They ate a large fruit salad for lunch: huge juicy slices of fresh pineapple and papaya, slivers of delicate melon, segments of sweet grapefruit and luscious pears. Joanna told Malika about the skimpy ham sandwich she would have been having in the doctors' dining-room at Moreton. 'Wait till I get back and tell them about this side of the world. It's like another planet.'

'You don't have to go back,' suggested Malika. 'Lots of people come here for a year and never go home. Look at Dr Bruce!'

'He came on a temporary basis too?'

'Sure did. He was staying with a friend, and the medico got sick, so Doc Bruce came for six months. Never went back to Jamaica.'

'But does he still own the plantation? Or are his parents still there?'

'No. His father died, and his mother sold up and went back to England, I think.'

'I wonder where?'

'You can always ask him.'

'Oh, no—he'd think I was prying. I'm not really interested in Dr Bruce.' She wondered if she ought to cross her fingers. It really was a very blatant lie.

Later, as they stood at the tennis courts, watching

some powerful practice by two beefy coaches slith-
ering, grunting and darting on the dusty red surface,
Malika said, 'You haven't told me what your fiancé
is like.'

Again Joanna was startled and concerned when
Roger's face didn't flash into her mind. Dash it, she
was going to be his wife. Surely she could describe
his appearance? 'Well, his hair is sort of brown-
ish. . .' It sounded disloyal to say it was already
thinning on top. That hadn't seemed important at
the time. But now, with her chief's magnificent head
of glossy white-blond locks catching their attention
every time he came to work, she felt it was too much
of a contrast to mention.

Malika laughed. 'Is that all?'

'And—grey eyes.' Serious eyes, that didn't light
up when she came into the room. Eyes that showed
Roger's concentration on his research into growth
hormone treatment for abnormally small children.
He only got animated when he had discovered
something interesting in his line of work. 'Steady.'
Yes, he was steady. Reliable. Full of integrity. Loyal
to his colleagues. 'Oh, gosh, Malika—I haven't
written to him. I must go and do it now.'

'We have to walk back past the polo field. You
don't mind if we watch them practising for a moment
or two?'

Joanna shook her head. 'No, naturally, a minute
or two doesn't matter.' She added slyly, 'Especially
if Señor Valentino is playing.'

No one knew Valentino's real name. There was
no denying his likeness to the silent film star—the
narrow lean face, the brooding dark eyes under

black brows, the languid way he looked at women as though expecting them to fall at his feet. And his polo uniform of breeches and leather boots emphasised his similarity to a desert sheikh.

Valentino was playing. And as the two girls stood among other hotel guests watching the practice game, he spotted Malika, and actually came over during a break in the game, smouldering down at them from the back of a glossy chestnut pony. '*Hola, Malika. Como está*?'

'*Muy bien*, Tino. Meet our new doctor, Joanna Bliss.'

Valentino favoured Joanna with his full frontal smile, and transferred his whip to the other hand in order to lean down and shake hands. 'Maybe now I will get sick more quickly!'

Joanna blushed. She wasn't used to the open admiration the men on Hernandez were not slow to express. Malika said pertly, 'Why now? I was always there at the medical centre!'

'Oh, you, Malika—I meet you every day! Is no novelty any more.'

Joanna stared at such tactlessness, but Malika's broad smile showed that it was a joke, and she had taken no offence. The whistle blew, and Tino raised his whip in salute before galloping back to the centre of the field. Joanna noticed that several of the guests were looking with envy at them. She thought again of Roger. With dashing young men apparently all around them at the Palacio, she knew she had to stop finding them attractive, and renew her relationship with Roger. 'I must get back and write that letter, Malika. You stay.'

But Malika came with her. 'I joke with him all the time. But I wouldn't like him to think I was serious.'

'I thought you were serious about him?'

'I am. I and about a hundred others! He won't settle down, Joanna. He's enjoying life too much.' Malika paused. 'And I don't want to be hurt.' She looked away. Her pretty dark face was thoughtful suddenly.

Joanna sat in the garden to write her letter. Think of Roger. Think of what a good man he is. Think of the thrill when he asked you to marry him, she thought. She spent some time giving herself a talking to, trying to put herself in the right mood to write the perfect letter.

'My dear Roger—a very beautiful country—hotel is quite nice——' It wouldn't do to sound too thrilled with the place. She tore up the page and started again. 'I work harder than I expected because my boss is a bit of an absentee. . .' No need to mention Dan Bruce—Roger might think things. No need to even say she worked with a man. 'I enjoy the work. It's excellent training for GP work. The children are very fit, with only the usual ailments. . .' She stopped, and remembered the families she had passed on the mountains, the naked children and the broken-down hovels. 'I hope to find time to look round the island, once I've got used to the routine at the medical centre.'

It was more difficult than she thought. However, she put together a letter of sorts. Then, to finish? All my love. . . With much love. . . Your loving. . . Joanna sat back, appalled at her inability to express her feelings to Roger. He was to be her husband.

They were to have children together. She gazed out over the sunlit garden. She could hear the cheerful voices of a party of golfers close by, the little buzz of their electric buggies. With a hasty scrawl, she wrote 'All my love, Joanna', and folded it quickly so that she wouldn't have second thoughts.

There was a bleep from the medical centre just before seven. Joanna was reading a book on skin problems in general practice that she had brought with her. Dermatology was one of her weaker subjects. She wasn't sorry to put the book down, give her hair a quick brush, and walk briskly across the gardens. There in the foyer stood Pete Marshall, chatting to Malika. He looked sheepish. 'It isn't a medical problem. I wondered if you'd have dinner with me. Malika said you wouldn't mind being paged, seeing as I'm heading for home tomorrow.'

'Of course I don't mind. I've checked Paul thoroughly, and he's fit to travel. The airline will have to give him a seat near the aisle, that's all, and look after his crutches.'

'I've rung them up. Pan-Am say there's no problem.'

No problem—the Hernandean motto. Joanna smiled. 'Then let's go.'

As they walked out into the dusk, with the fairy lights twinkling in the trees, and the distant music pulsing through the walkways, Pete said, 'I'm only sorry you haven't had a day off since we met. I'd have liked to drive you out into the country. Have you seen much of the scenery?'

'Not much.' She laughed. 'You'll think I'm crazy,

Pete, but I haven't even checked to see when I do have some time off.'

'You must love your work some.'

'Maybe I do. It's different, anyway.' Yet it wasn't different work. The illnesses and the pain were the same. It was Hernandez that made the difference— to be surrounded by warmth and beauty and luxury, that made the difference. Joanna knew that if she weren't very careful it might prove to be addictive, as both Señor Riaz and Dan Bruce had warned her.

He had hired a car, and they drove along to Constanza, where a small café called Camilo's was lit with flickering candles. 'I hope you like this place,' said Pete. 'I discovered it after one of my walks to the experimental fields. Got chatting to one of the guys about agriculture, and he brought me here. The food in the hotel complex is great. But this is the real Hernandez, for my money.'

'I know what you mean. In the hotel you don't meet the people. You meet those who are paid to make you comfortable. But you can't find out any genuine opinions there.' Joanna took the menu handed to her by a smiling Camilo. He was dressed in simple T-shirt and jeans. There was no fancy décor, just wooden tables with checked cloths, a delicious savoury smell coming from the back, and a small bar in the corner. '*Gracias*,' she said.

They had vegetable soup in earthenware bowls, with freshly baked bread. Then Pete said, 'If you have no ethical reasons against it, I recommend the *chivo a la criolla*.'

'It sounds OK,' said Joanna warily. 'What is it?'

'Try it. Tell me if you think it's good.' Steaming

plates of rice and meat were placed before them. It was tender and quite delicious. 'It's actually goat,' Pete told her, when she had pronounced it excellent.

'Oh!'

He smiled. His face was open and honest, his eyes direct. 'You know, Joanna, I haven't known you very long. But I'm going to miss you.'

'It always happens on holiday. You always miss some things.' She was touched by his admission. She recalled Dan Bruce telling her that Pete was smitten. She said quickly, 'I miss my fiancé. But it's fun to meet new people.'

'I'm going to try and get back here before your year is up.'

She, smiled and tried to shrug off his youthful admiration. 'I'll still be engaged to be married, Pete.'

He grinned then. 'And we could still go dancing! How about it? A last dance down by the main pool?'

'All right.' She surprised herself by her ready answer. When he had first invited her to dance, she had felt guilty about Roger. Now she hadn't given him more than a thought. After all, their love was strong enough to stand a year's separation. It would make it all the more pleasant when she got back to Moreton, to a stable home life, to have happy memories to look back on.

They danced until after midnight. At first the band played rhythmic popular Caribbean music, which made Joanna want to dance in time to the drums and the maraccas. But as the night wore on they played slow *salsa* music, and her young companion held her close, and showed sadness at having to let her go when the music stopped. 'I'll walk you back?' he offered.

'No, Pete, let's say goodbye here.'

He gave a rueful smile. 'OK, ma'am. It's been great knowing you. I'll be thinking of you.' And he leaned over and kissed her cheek lingeringly. 'Thanks for all you did for Paul.'

'Goodnight, Pete. Good luck.'

As he walked away, he stopped and turned round, calling gently, 'I might write—just to let you know how Paul is getting on.'

Joanna didn't answer. But she was smiling to herself as she walked slowly back to the villa in the warm darkness. It was like being young again, like her first years at medical school. Hernandez, she thought, I think I love you.

CHAPTER FIVE

IT WAS some days later. Joanna still had not had a full day off, although the weekends were very quiet, and she found herself spending the time just like the other hotel guests. She introduced herself to the tennis coaches, and played a few games in the sun. Then she discovered the health lodge, and treated herself to a massage and sauna, finishing off with a dip in the nearest pool.

Malika wasn't on duty at weekends, and her position at the desk was taken by one of the receptionists from the main hotel. Her name was Juanita. She was Spanish, and made no secret of her crush on Dan Bruce. 'I would work for him for nothing,' she crooned to Joanna, introducing herself. 'Have you ever met such a sexy man?'

Joanna couldn't help laughing—partly to hide her own embarrassment. 'I don't notice things like that. I'm a doctor!'

'You don't tell me that doctors have no feelings?'

'Well, they do, of course. But I have a fiancé back in England,' Joanna explained.

'Huh!' The exuberant brunette lifted her hands in disbelief. 'A hundred fiancés couldn't make Dr Bruce invisible! Oh, if only he were on duty today while I am here!'

'Sorry about the disappointment,' said Joanna, amused. 'But shall I take a look at that patient now?'

'Sorry, sorry.' Juanita was entertaining in her expressions of regret. 'I didn't mean to hurt your feelings, Doctor. I bring in the girl now.'

Joanna went to her consulting-room, while Juanita filled out a card with the patient's details, and ushered her in. 'This is Señorita Frances Meadows.'

The girl was about twenty, pretty in a slim, demure way. But Joanna noticed at once that she was pale under her suntan, sweating, and her eyes seemed to be disappearing between swollen lids. Some allergic reaction, obviously. 'What is it, Frances? Lie on the couch, please, while I examine you.'

'It's a silly thing, Doctor.' The girl was Canadian, and had a gentle drawl to her speech. 'I was stung. It was only a small wasp, and only one sting. Surely that can't make me feel as dreadful as this?'

'It can, I'm afraid, if you're sensitive to the substance in the sting.' Joanna listened to heart and lungs, then took the blood-pressure. It was low. 'Is your blood pressure usually low?'

'Normal, I guess. No one's ever said otherwise.'

'Then I'd better give you an antihistamine right now by injection.' There was no point in alarming the patient unduly, but Joanna had known a case like this when the patient had died from an extreme reaction. She rang the bell for the nurse. 'Get a bed ready, please. I just want to give this lady an injection, but if she doesn't improve within half an hour, she may need hydrocortisone.'

They made the girl comfortable in a hospital room. 'I'll stay here at the centre until I'm sure she's all right,' Joanna decided, and went back to her consulting-room. It was almost five in the afternoon, and she was feeling tired after a strenuous game of tennis with one of the physiotherapists from the health lodge. Juanita came in with a cup of iced lemon tea. 'Thanks, Juanita. That's just what I could do with.'

'I come to tell you Dr Bruce is back,' said Juanita.

'He can't be. Not when he isn't on duty.'

Then a voice from the doorway showed her how wrong she was. 'Wishful thinking, Doctor!'

She sat up sharply. He was lounging in the doorway, dressed in tennis shirt and grey flannels. She said faintly, 'Good evening, Doctor.' She saw Juanita watching them carefully, alert to any sign of intimacy between them. She knew too that Juanita was the sort of cheerful gossip who could spread a rumour in a place like this in record time. 'Well, it's nice to see you, but I have no time to chat. I must get back to the ward.' She stood up.

'What about your tea, Doctor?' He was teasing her very openly, and she knew she mustn't rise to the bait. Especially with Juanita present.

She made her voice cool. 'Of course. The shock of finding you at work when you don't need to be drove everything else out of my head.' She picked up the cup and saucer and sipped the tea with as much composure as she could manage.

Dan was smiling, and his eyes were very blue as the light began to fade, and rays of the setting sun penetrated the slatted blinds. But he somehow sensed the need for propriety, and to her great relief said nothing but, 'I'll be in my room for half an hour. There's some paperwork to do.' And he left the room, somehow taking some of the sunlight with him.

Juanita stood, her eyes dewy. 'I will take him some tea also,' she said, and drifted from the room. Joanna sat down hard, and put her head in her hands. It required a lot of extra nervous energy, working with a man of such open and powerful sensuality. She wondered why he had left his woman so early tonight. This was the first time he had turned up at the medical centre without warning. His very unpredictability was exasperating. She was glad she had work to do, walking along to Frances Meadows's room to see if the antihistamine had taken effect.

The girl was still in slight shock. A nurse was sitting with her, and had put on a small lamp, as the sun had set, and the crickets outside were chirping lustily as night fell. Joanna picked up a phial of hydrocortisone and drew some off into a syringe. She felt for a vein on the girl's arm, and slowly injected the drug. Then she sat on the bed, waiting. Within minutes the effects began to be obvious. First the girl's eyes opened more easily, as the puffiness began to disappear. Within fifteen minutes her colour was better, and, when Joanna took her blood-pressure with the nurse's sphyg, it was back to a healthy hundred and twenty over seventy-five.

'Is anyone with you, Miss Meadows?'

'I'm with a group of girls. I didn't tell them I was coming here.'

'I'll get a message to them. I think you ought to stay in overnight.'

'Thank you, Doctor. I never even thought a simple sting could be so dangerous.'

'Before you leave tomorrow, I'll make sure you have some antihistamine cream,' Joanna told her. 'And as you're so very sensitive, a course of tablets would be advisable.'

The girl said, 'I was quite scared, actually. I had such a tightness in my throat.'

Joanna nodded. 'So was I. That was the worst symptom.' That was what she had feared most. 'We'll make sure it doesn't happen again.'

She tried to leave quietly. She had been successful in avoiding Dan Bruce for the past week or so, and her equilibrium had come back, with no close encounters, or even occasions where the two of them were alone together. It was the best course of action.

But Juanita spoiled it by calling, 'Goodnight, Dr Bliss!'

'Goodnight, Juanita.' In contrast to Juanita's cheerful call, Joanna almost whispered her farewell. She heard Dan's door open, and she ran.

Some time later, as she sat on the wall where she could see the starlit beach, and hear the lapping of the waves on the sand, Joanna began to think she had been silly not to go straight home. How could she be so vain as to think Dan Bruce would follow her there? That was why she had come here, to escape being alone with him. And that was why she was now very hungry indeed.

She edged herself off the wall and stood up. Then she turned round towards the hotel. Blocking her sight of it was Dan Bruce, hands on hips. She drew in her breath with a sudden gasp. Then, to hide her embarrassment at being scared, she said angrily, 'Isn't that a bit pointless? Standing in the dark without saying anything?'

He said quietly, 'And isn't it pointless sitting in the dark all by yourself?'

She started to walk away, but he caught her arm and stopped her. She replied coldly, 'You may be my boss, but away from work you can't control my every waking minute, Dan.'

There was a silence between them. The sea washed the shore and the crickets sang. Then he said, 'You said it, Joanna. You finally said it.'

'What?'

'My name.'

'Oh, that.' A mistake. She didn't mean to. 'So what?'

'Nothing. I only came to ask you to play tennis with me. The coach says you're quite good.'

'You could have asked that tomorrow. We can't very well play now.'

'We can play all night if we want to. With the floodlights. Look.' And in the distance she could see the strip lighting around the tennis courts.

'Well, I'm too hungry.'

'Good. Then let's eat. We can arrange the match over dinner.'

'I'm not having dinner with you.'

'Who, then?'

'Alone.' She started to walk back towards the hotel, and he fell into step beside her. 'I mean it.'

'OK.' They walked a few more paces. Then he said, 'Have you ever thought why the local villagers don't get violent prophylactic shock when they get stung?'

'Like Miss Meadows, you mean? I suppose they're born with immunity. A lot of people are. Otherwise we'd all get hay fever for a start.'

'Would you like to see a study that's been done in Constanza?'

'Very much. I've been wondering who looks after the poor people—the ones who live in wooden shacks, and have no running water. What do they do if they're ill? Who looks after the mothers when they give birth?'

'Either the local government hospitals—which are more like concrete shacks themselves—or the witch woman,' Dan told her.

'What?'

He stopped, and they faced each other. He said quietly, 'You've heard of voodoo, no doubt.'

'Gosh!' Suddenly Joanna knew she was in the Caribbean. The ocean and the flowers, the palm trees and the smooth tropical air—they could be found in many places. But not everywhere was there a link with a violent, troubled history, of African slaves and their mystical gods and sacrifices.

Dan said, 'I'll tell you about it over dinner.'

'No—thank you.'

He said, 'Not like last time. I shouldn't have come back to the villa last time. I'm sorry.'

'It's still no.' He might have started it last time— the kissing. But Joanna knew very well it was she who had encouraged it. She who had not wanted it to stop. It was herself she was afraid of, not Dan Bruce.

After ten minutes, during which they walked through the hotel and round the gardens, Dan said, 'Are you trying to shake me off, Joanna?'

'No. Just walking.'

'Where are you having dinner?'

The mention of food made her even more hungry. 'I haven't decided yet.'

'Then how about in here?' And he held her arm gently, and guided her to an open-sided restaurant set among hibiscus bushes, adjoining a small wooden dance-floor, where a trio of drummer, trumpet player and saxophone played mood music under frangipani trees set like stars with their fragrant white flowers. Joanna sat down. There were limits to one's resistance, when one was as hungry as she was. Dan spoke quietly to the waiter, not asking her what she wanted. And shortly a silver ice bucket containing a bottle of white wine was set beside them, and two plates of something that looked like curry placed before them. He smiled, and poured the wine. '*Salud*!'

She raised her glass to him in return, still embarrassed by his keen eyes that seemed to read her soul, and to understand how afraid she was that she might lose her self-control again. '*Salud*. But I still think it would be better for us to maintain a strictly business relationship.'

'Whatever else is this?'

'I mean. . .' He seemed to take pleasure in her discomfort. She went on bravely, 'Not to meet out of work.'

Dan leaned back in his chair for a moment, regarding her with amused eyes. 'Joanna, my dear, if your relationship with your fiancé isn't strong enough to withstand the occasional dinner with your boss, then I feel you ought to rethink the whole thing. You either love the man and want no one else but him—or you've made a bad mistake, in which case it's better to find it out sooner rather than after you've actually promised to love and obey.'

'I didn't know you were a marriage guidance counsellor as well as your other accomplishments.'

He reached for his fork, and smiled at her. 'What accomplishments?'

'The ability never to be at work when you're needed.'

He didn't answer for a while, as they both ate. It was one of the best meals she had ever tasted. When their first hunger had been assuaged, Dan said, 'You know the answer to that. You're employed to be my shadow. When I'm not there—you are. It's as simple as that, and we've already discussed it.'

It was Joanna's turn to smile. 'Don't get touchy, Dan. I know we discussed it. But you did ask me what your accomplishments were, and I can't think of anything else.'

And then the bleep went off in her pocket. Dan put his hand on hers. 'Don't get up. Finish your turtle. I'll see to this one. I've finished eating.'

'Turtle!' She looked at the cubes of tasty meat with new eyes. When she looked up, Dan had gone. She sat back, smiling inside. She must have got through to him. He had answered the pager in exasperation at her nagging. He had to prove that he wasn't always an absentee. She finished the meal slowly, then went back to the villa, glad that she didn't have to fight him off this time. It made life much simpler, staying apart.

But when the bleep sounded next time, it was three-thirty in the morning, and she had been asleep only four hours. She rubbed her eyes hard to wake herself up, and dressed quickly in a shirt, jeans and sandals. The night nurse was waiting for her. 'Dr Bruce's patient. He admitted her at eight last evening.'

'Yes, I was with him when you called.'

'He said it was biliary colic. The patient's pain settled, but she's rolling in agony just now, and I don't know where Dr Bruce is.'

Joanna frowned. 'There's no way we can operate tonight. Let's see if we can get her comfortable.' She gave the patient, a middle-aged woman, an analgesic injection, which quieted her temporarily. She tried Dan's telephone again, but he had obviously gone to his lady friend in town, and was incommunicado. She rang Dr Jamis. 'I've made the patient comfortable,' she told him.

'But you don't want to tackle a cholecystectomy?'

'I certainly don't feel happy.'

'I'll see what I can do. Maybe I can get the general surgeon from the town hospital. I'll call you back, Joanna.' And after a few minutes Dr Jamis rang back. 'The surgeon can't make it. But surely Dan will be back in the morning? If we get theatre ready for nine-thirty, he can take over.'

'Very well, we'll schedule it for nine-thirty. Thank you, Doctor.' After all, it was Dan's night off. No one could blame him for not being available. Joanna dragged herself back to bed. She was tired, but the thought of having to do a major operation worried her, and she lay awake, going over and over in her mind the main arteries in the area that could bleed, and the best procedure for removing a gall bladder. It should be straightforward. But she hadn't done more than a senior houseman's six months in surgery, and had only ever seen three operations on the gall bladder in that time.

She was gowned, gloved and masked by nine-fifteen. The patient had been prepped, and lay, semi-conscious, as the pre-med injection began to work. Please don't let Dan be late today, she prayed. But her prayers were silent, and she presented a confident exterior to the theatre staff, and to the patient.

He was five minutes late, then ten. Joanna knew she couldn't delay any longer—especially when there were out-patients waiting for the normal morning clinic. 'OK, let's go.' She quietly checked the instruments, noting with relief that her hand wasn't shaking. 'Right. Let's start.'

Dr Jamis, at the patient's head, gave her a thumbs-up with a gloved thumb. She made a generous incision over the costal margin, drew back the flaps of skin, and took a deep breath. But she hesitated. This was a human being, unconscious on the table. Had she the right to proceed, while aware of her own lack of experience? She knew it was foolish to go on like this. She said, 'Hold it there, please, Nurse,' and left the theatre.

Dan was there, in gown and cap, hastily thrusting his feet into theatre boots. 'It's OK,' he told her. 'Come on, we'll do it together.'

'I—panicked a bit.' She was ashamed of it, but knew it was right to admit it.

'No problem, Joanna.' The two doctors went back into theatre together, and Dan took her place while she stood opposite to assist. Gradually the offending organ was removed, the arteries cauterised, the wound closed. And gradually, too, Joanna's gratitude turned to anger. Why wasn't he here when he was supposed to be? It was downright dereliction of duty, to leave a junior to shoulder the responsibility of major surgery.

They undressed in silence, and she drew the curtain of the cubicle to put on her day clothes. Her anger simmered. Dan sauntered into the waiting area and nodded calmly at Malika. 'Send in the first patient, my dear,' he told her.

Joanna went to her consulting-room. But it was no good. She was furious with Dan for being late when it mattered so much. She rang her bell, and Malika came running. 'Ready for your first patient, Joanna?'

'No. They can all see Dr bloody Bruce. I'm going home!'

Malika stared with wide brown eyes. Joanna had never shown any temper before. Not like this. She had blown up at Dan—but that was in the past, wasn't it? 'Sure, Joanna. I'll tell him.' She went to the door. 'Will I see you at the beach later?'

'I'm not sure. You might.' Joanna picked up her bag, took out the pager, banged it down on her desk, and swept from the building into the hot mid-morning sun. It wasn't fair to treat Malika like that. But the combination of not enough sleep, plus the anxiety of knowing she could have made a serious mistake, was taking its toll, and she had to get right away for a while, to regain her composure.

She left her things at the villa, then spoke briefly to Rosita, who was polishing the parquet floor till it shone. 'I'm just taking a walk,' she said.

'Want me to cook anything for lunch?' asked Rosita.

'No, thank you.'

She walked along the beach, past the holiday-makers, the swimmers, water-skiers, even the bird-watchers. She left the hotel guests far behind and wandered along the coast where it was more rocky and wild, and where she could be alone. She sat on a rock and stared out to the glittering sea until her eyes hurt. Then she lay back under a palm tree and closed her eyes. She fell asleep.

When she opened her eyes, she felt calmer. The sun had shifted from left to right in the blue sky, and fluffy clouds decorated it like wisps of cotton wool. Then she sat up very straight. Dan Bruce was sitting with his back to her on a rock closer to the sea, staring out. Tension snapped back into her body, and showed in her voice. 'What are you doing here?' she demanded.

'I thought you might like to explain.' He turned, and hooked his bare brown arms round one knee.

'I don't see there is anything to explain.'

'I thought we understood one another. You're here to cover for me. You said you understood that.'

'Cover is one thing, Doctor. Being left in a potentially dangerous situation is quite another. You were expected at nine-thirty. You didn't arrive at nine-thirty, and you didn't let us know where you were. I think I'm entitled to be annoyed—especially as I had to get up in the night to see your patient. You hadn't left any instructions with the night nurse about analgesics.'

'Right. Now you've got that off your chest, shall we get back? There's a woman in labour in the hospital—one of the maids. She has pre-eclampsia, and I'd be grateful for your assistance.'

Joanna rose to her feet and brushed the sand from the skirt of her dress. 'Why didn't you say? I'll get back, then.'

Dan was on his feet in a moment, and walking alongside her. 'You reckon you could cope alone?'

'With pre-eclampsia, yes, if the birth is straightforward. Why?'

'Because I ought to be somewhere else, but I couldn't go in case my assistant got stroppy again and walked out on me.' His voice was cold now. Joanna clenched her fists. It was his fault she was angry, yet he was trying to make her feel guilty.

She quickened her step to try and get away from him, but he merely lengthened his stride and kept level. 'Dan Bruce, you can be a real bastard!' She knew she shouldn't have said it. But Dan's stride never faltered, and they arrived at the medical centre together. Her face was flaming with the exertion, with the sun, and with the emotion of hating someone. He walked in before her and didn't hold the door open.

CHAPTER SIX

IT WAS November, and Joanna had been working at
the Palacio Hotel for four months. It was a good
life, better than it had been in her grim little home
town. She was on Christian-name terms with many
of the staff, and had made some good friends among
the guests.

Her boss was less predictable, but she expected
nothing else. After their last quarrel in August—the
only time she had ever missed a surgery—they had
been polite to each other, but wary. Neither had
referred to it again, and the routine of the medical
centre went on, with Joanna shouldering most of the
work, but with Dan turning up in the mornings, and
occasionally going missing in the afternoons and
nights.

She had mentioned to Roger briefly that she was
working with another doctor 'who doesn't always
turn up, but this gives me a chance to gain more
experience, and confidence, which I know will prove
useful when I come home.'

She was chatting to Malika and Juanita about the
approaching Christmas festivities. 'You will love the
Palacio then, Joanna,' they told her. 'We have
famous international musicians, and concerts and
fancy dress balls. Whatever the guests have, the staff
are welcome to join in. You'll love it.'

'And Christmas Day itself?'

'The medical centre staff are all given a holiday. They get young doctors from the town hospital who are glad of the extra money to come in and look after emergencies.'

Juanita said, 'We go to the beach, Joanna, and have a barbecue. You will come, won't you? We all help—bring different things for the feast.'

'Does Dr Bruce——?'

'He came last year. Oh, Joanna, what a body in his swimming trunks! Didn't stay long enough, though. Off to his lady-love, I suppose.' Juanita laughed. 'What can we poor lovesick staff expect? At least we all got a kiss from him!'

Joanna bit her lip. She wished she didn't keep thinking of the night Dan had kissed her. To be aroused like that—to be on fire, to be beyond all thought in the honeyed wilds of her experience—it was shaming that she knew she was wishing it could happen again.

Dr Bruce pushed the door open. He wasn't expected. The three women all looked up, as the blond figure, reminding Joanna of a picture she had once seen of Sir Galahad, strode into the foyer, and stood, legs straddled, hands on hips. He was smiling. 'You girls are being paid far too much. All you do is stand around and gossip.' The receptionists giggled, and Joanna turned away.

Dan said, 'Dr Bliss, the old man over in the staff quarters has passed away. I was going over to comfort the daughter, and I remembered she'd taken a liking to you.'

'I didn't know.'

'She told me you'd been very patient with her. If you can spare the time——'

'Yes, Doctor.' She suppressed a remark about Dan being the one who could never spare the time. 'I'll go right away. Number seven, wasn't it? Top flat?'

'I'll come with you.'

'Oh, all right.' Her voice probably showed her reluctance to go with him. But a professional woman shouldn't let her feelings show. In any case, when they worked together there was seldom any disagreement. It was only out of work that the sparks flew.

Neither spoke, as they crossed the road to the staff flats. But Joanna was acutely aware of Dan's closeness, and also of the number of times she had remembered what it felt like to be close to him, to be held like a treasured being, and kissed as though it mattered. They went up to the top floor, where a little maid, still in her working pale blue gingham dress and white apron, sat dry-eyed but pathetic, over the body covered with a sheet. 'Take a week off, Nanda.' Joanna had gone straight to the girl, her professional being taking over from the woman underneath. 'He was a good man. It will leave a gap in your life, but it will heal. Think of the good times you had. And remember he's in a good place now. He's happy, my dear. Think that.'

'But I can't take time. No time to grieve, Doctor. The *Señora* will be angry if I am off work and I am not ill myself.'

'I'll give you a certificate. Go and stay with your aunt in the town.'

'She's coming as soon as she has finished work. She's his sister. Now we are both alone.'

Joanna was sad for the sister who couldn't come to her brother's dying because she was a maidservant, and she had the chores to complete before she was free to come out. The tradition of slavery hadn't quite gone in Hernandez, in spite of the democracy and the freedom. Money still made all the decisions. Joanna sighed. It was people's hearts that had to change, not the political system.

On the way back, Dan was still quiet. He walked with her past the medical centre. She said, her voice still hoarse after the emotion of the patient, 'I know the way home.'

'May I come for a cup of tea?' he asked quietly.

She looked at him with sudden respect. He was moved. It was well hidden, but she saw the tear on his cheek that he hid by shrugging his shoulder upwards, and catching the tear as it rolled. 'Yes. Sure.' It was a side of Dan Bruce he had never shown anyone before, and it disarmed her.

The tears were gone by the time she made tea, and carried it on a tray into her long, cool lounge. He said, 'Joanna, I'm a self-centred man. I don't need to tell you that, do I?'

Again there was something in his voice that stopped her telling him just how selfishly he had acted in the past. She said gently, 'No. No need even to mention it.'

'I'd just like to say that I do think of others sometimes. And I was right to ask you to come to Nanda. You did more good to her than I ever could.'

'Does she matter to you in some way?'

'No, not really.' He looked across, and she saw some tension in the way he sat on the edge of the chair, the way he kept moving his fingers on the arms of the chair. He said, 'To be honest, I didn't expect an English person to have so much caring in their nature.'

'You mean for a black woman?' she asked bluntly.

'Yes.'

She looked across the room at him. He had lowered his gaze, and the blue eyes were curtained. 'Maybe you should pay a visit to Britain some time,' she told him.

She handed him tea, and he sipped it without speaking for some time, so that she had leisure to steal glances at him, to think him even more handsome when his eyes were sad and thoughtful and sincere. He said finally, 'I'm really sorry we fought.'

Joanna said nothing. When Dan looked up and met her gaze, she said, 'So am I.'

There was a click, and they both turned as something slid through the letterbox on to the polished floor. 'Letter for you,' he said.

She didn't go right away. She wanted to stay in the cocoon of closeness that had been generated by their last words. 'I don't know much about you,' she admitted. 'Even though we've worked together for almost half a year.'

'Half a year? Not long till you leave us, then. Do you want to?'

'I was told I might not want to leave. The magic of Hernandez, and all that.'

He looked at her. 'It might still work.'

She smiled. 'Maybe.'

Dan put the cup down, and stood up. 'Well, Joanna, I've made such apologies as I can.'

'I appreciate it.'

'See you tomorrow, then.'

'Right.' She stood up too, and walked to the door with him. He bent and picked up the letter, handed it to her. She recognised Roger's spidery ball-point, and put the letter on the hall table.

'Boyfriend?'

'Yes.'

'I don't suppose——' Dan turned away, and Joanna reached up to open the door for him. He caught her hand before she touched the latch. 'Could we have dinner?'

It was wrong, and probably foolish. But when she was this close, his warmth and smell sent her common sense out of sync. She said, 'I was just going to say it would be a good idea. Sort of peace-offering. I've said some things to you that I regret.'

With a rustle of his cotton shirt, she found herself in his arms, her head on his chest, feeling right to be there, to be held, to be comforting each other. He didn't kiss her, though she felt his hand stroking her hair. They just stood, holding each other very close, feeling the beating of two hearts. After a while Dan murmured, 'We've got half a year to put things right, then?'

'Sure.'

'I'll come and pick you up in an hour.'

'Yes.'

It was a chance to wear the third of her new dresses, the prettiest, and the one she had pushed to the back of the wardrobe in her first rush of disappointment when she had found out how unreliable and autocratic Dan was. She was beginning to see a glimmer of another side to him, a more caring, emotional side. A side that he hadn't shown to Malika or to Juanita. It was too soon to say it was friendship—but the signs were there that a new closeness might develop.

Joanna luxuriated in a long bath. She washed her hair and fluffed it out about her suntanned face. How well and healthy she looked now. Dan had called her beautiful once. Maybe, in some lights, and when she was happy, as she was now, it could be true. She slipped on the silk dress, a subtle mix of dark green and dark blue, with touches of black. It rustled against her bare legs, and made her feel desirable. She felt herself blushing, to even think such a thing when she owed allegiance to her fiancé, not to the man she was to meet in fifteen minutes.

Fiancé! She had completely forgotten Roger's letter. Guiltily she went out to the hall and slit open the envelope. Then she sat down with shock. Roger was coming to Hernandez for Christmas! 'I find myself with two weeks' holiday I must take before March,' he had written. 'The research is going well, but naturally I can't expect to see patients over the Christmas season, so I've booked to fly out to Miami on the fourteenth of December, and catch a connecting flight to Hernandez City. I don't expect you to meet me—I see from the map it's a long way from Constanza. I'll telephone you when I arrive.' And he ended with uncharacteristic affection, 'I miss you, Joanna, more than I expected I would.'

The front door bell rang. Dan! Roger's words had completely destroyed her mood of happy anticipation, and she shoved the letter swiftly into a drawer. She ought not to be going. What if Roger came early, and found her wining and dining with an attractive man—a man with a million times more sex appeal than Roger, if the truth were told. . .? Waves of guilt and worry enveloped her. As she opened the door, she felt her heart stir with something like desire at Dan's tall figure, with his neat dark trousers, expensive shirt and tie, and that mass of fair hair outlined against the dark of the night studded with coloured lights. It would be folly to be alone with him tonight.

'I can't come,' she told him shortly.

He didn't react—just stood, with a slight smile in those clear blue eyes. 'An attack of conscience after reading his letter?'

'Yes,' she said directly.

'Then let's call it a business meeting. I want to discuss money matters with you.'

'I'm only an employee.'

'Don't make excuses, Joanna. You have a brain, haven't you? You have an opinion? On most things a very definite opinion.'

'That's true.'

'Then could we go? I'm getting hungry.'

She emerged from the shelter of the front door, checking that the pager was in her patent leather shoulderbag that went so well with the silk dress. 'I mustn't be late,' she told him.

'Of course, *señorita*.' He was teasing her, but it sounded so lovely to be called *señorita* in such a sweet accent. As she closed the door, his eyes were appreciative. 'My dear, you look far too lovely to be a doctor. I'm promoting you to the Hernandean royalty tonight. Princesa Joanna.'

His gentleness began to dissipate her guilt, and she laughed. 'Oh, good. Then for once I shall be your superior, and if the pager goes—you go!'

'Ah, no, I didn't tell you—the pager breaks the spell and demotes you instantly!' And, laughing, Dan took her arm, linking his through it in a familiar and totally delightful, informal way—as though they were real friends. 'Have you eaten in Constanza, *princesa*?'

'Yes—I've been to Camilo's.'

'That's a good place. But I know a better—on the outskirts. We'll take the car.' And he drove out of the hotel complex, both doctors being saluted respectfully by the uniformed commissionaires at the great wide gates, which were more elegant than those of any real palace Joanna had seen in Britain. The road became dark, away from the Palacio, and the headlights lit up wild tamarinds, sleeping white hump-backed cattle, and the neatly laid out fields of spiky pineapples and new-planted rice.

'What a place!' breathed Joanna. And she remembered Roger again, and wondered how he would fit in, among all this excitingly different scenery and people.

'What are you thinking?'

She said quietly, 'Roger is coming.'

The car swerved very slightly, as Dan's fingers gripped the wheel more tightly. 'When?' She told him. 'I see.' He sounded reserved, suddenly. 'I look

forward to meeting him. Child health, you said?
Maybe he could give us some advice about our
vaccination programme.'

'He'd be very interested. His pet subject is growth
hormone treatment at the moment. I suppose that
doesn't exist on Hernandez?'

'For the rich, Joanna, everything exists. We're
only four hours from the States, remember.'

'I realise that.'

'When you write back, tell Roger—what's his
second name?'

'Fordham.'

'Tell Dr Fordham I look forward to meeting him.'

Joanna was silent. She wasn't sure what Roger's
reaction would be to finding that her boss in the
Palacio was just about the most virile and attractive
male next to young Valentino in the entire complex.
And that included the golf pros and the tennis
coaches! It wasn't something that she wanted to tell
Roger about.

They drew up beside what looked like a barn.
Almost before they had stepped out of the car, a
couple of young boys were there, with bucket and
leathers, waiting to clean the car. 'They need every
centavo they can earn, just to live,' Dan told her.
'They come from those shacks you passed when you
came through the mountains.'

The hovels: one-roomed sheds, with no water,
and a wood stove outside to do the cooking. Joanna
felt deep compassion, but helplessness because there
was nothing she could do to change things for these
people. 'I've just lost my appetite.'

'Oh, no—you have to eat. By starving yourself

you only make the restaurant owner go out of business.'

Joanna couldn't help smiling. 'I've never met anyone with all the answers before. You're never at a loss for words, are you, Dan?'

He paused at the door, looked back at her before he opened the door to usher her in before him. 'Almost never, *princesa*.'

Hypnotised by the beauty of his blue gaze, she didn't take much notice of the surroundings. The restaurant was a copy of the usual village dwellings, wood-framed and thatched-roofed, with bare rafters supporting dim electric lamps. There were several other Hernandean couples, one family with two well-behaved children, already eating. Dan was received with cordiality, and Joanna with admiration. Again she allowed Dan to order for her. The head waiter came over to light the candle on their table, and hand Joanna a red rose, its long stem wrapped in silver foil.

'This is a bit romanticised, Dan,' she protested. 'Can't you tell them that it's only a business meeting?'

'Don't spoil it for them,' he grinned. 'I might be about to propose to you. They only provide the atmosphere! They're doing their best.'

Joanna felt her face flush. Even in fun, the idea of Dan wanting to marry her filled her with prickly embarrassment. And reminded her that the man she was truly going to marry was already probably packing his mosquito repellant and buying tropical drill shorts. 'You said you wanted to talk about money.' But Dan was ordering Cuba *libres*, and didn't seem to hear her.

Plates of savoury deliciousness were placed before them. Joanna didn't ask what it was. She was already feeling a sense of loss, because when Roger arrived she wouldn't be able to mix as freely with her colleague. And she knew it was wrong to feel such deprivation. If Roger mattered so much, why wasn't she delighted?

He was looking at her, his eyes apparently reading her thoughts again. 'The Cuba *libre* OK?'

Joanna had to smile. 'Apparently, yes. I seem to be one of the lucky ones, getting a lesson in mixing drinks from the expert himself.'

He leaned on his elbows and looked into her eyes. 'Be honest, *princesa*. It's fun finding out about Hernandez from me.'

She did her best to remain calm. No point in admitting anything. Even though the man was telling the truth, it was infuriating. Roger Fordham was on his way, almost. And if Joanna had any honour in her, she had to remember she had given Roger her promise. She said, 'I'm an honest person, Dan. And life is rather too much fun at the moment. Please understand my position. The Palacio job has been fantastic, but it's only temporary. I mustn't lose sight of that. Life couldn't possibly be so much fun indefinitely.'

'Why not?'

'Well—it just can't.'

'Joanna, it could, you know.'

His voice was so tender, so very husky and sincere. She clutched her throat, making sure that she didn't say anything that would give away her emotions, which seemed to be under Dan's control just then. Joanna tried to look at him objectively. 'You're trying to manipulate me, Dan Bruce,' she complained.

'Then forgive me—it isn't intentional. But at the moment I can't visualise a medical centre without you. Next year will be like a desert.'

Music started up in the background. A recording of one of the top bands in the country, as Malika had taught Joanna. She said, recognising them, 'Ah, Cinco-Cincuenta!'

He smiled broadly at her knowledge. 'Then let's dance, *princesa*.'

At that moment, one of the couples who had been sitting in a corner danced past them. Joanna looked up, thinking that the woman was extraordinarily pretty. Straight, glossy short hair, and a wonderfully mobile face, with smooth skin and full, generous lips. She was slim, and wore a slinky creation of cream satin. She stopped, pulling her partner up abruptly. 'Dan, darling—how wonderful!' Her accent was cut-glass English, tinkling with reminders of weekend shoots, Ascot and coming-out balls.

Dan half rose in recognition. The couple danced past, and he sat down again. 'A dentist I know,' he explained to Joanna. 'Quite good, actually.'

Joanna wasn't surprised. Dan Bruce had always given the impression of being uncommitted to the medical centre. She felt a tingle of certainty. This beautiful woman was surely the reason for Dan's constant absenteeism. Quite by chance, his secret had come out. 'Oh, really?' She knew she had

maintained a totally uninterested attitude. Her voice
had been cool, polite. But Dan Bruce couldn't know
just how far away in light years Joanna felt from the
brittle debutante who had danced past them, shapely
hips swinging, and pricey shoes twinkling in time
with the band.

They sat down. The magic of the evening had
vanished. Dan said, 'Quite a surprise, meeting
Melanie.'

'Melanie.' Joanna repeated the name without
emotion. Melanie was quite lovely. Beautiful, in
fact. But it was a shock, meeting so unexpectedly
the woman who had charmed Dan away from his
duties so often, and so consistently. Joanna looked
across the table, trying to read her escort's face. 'So
at last I see why I've been doing so much extra
work!' she remarked.

'I beg your pardon?'

He did seem nonplussed. Joanna didn't repeat the
statement. Dan was his own boss. Just inviting her
out didn't mean anything at all. She had no hold
over Dan. But she did wish that his secret love had
stayed secret. Now she knew what Melanie looked
like. She could think of her at night, when Dan
wasn't available on the pager, knowing exactly
where he was, what he was doing, and who with. . .

Dan reached across the table and put his hand
over Joanna's. 'Dance?'

'All right.' There was little else she could say. Dan
might be in love with the glamorous dentist, but he
was with Joanna at that moment, and she had a
strange feeling of loss. His arms were round her, and
his eyes were on her as they danced. If Melanie had

not been there, it would have been romantic and rapturous, an evening when she could have again forgotten temporarily her promises to Roger, and enjoyed the physical closeness Dan Bruce offered so freely. They swayed to the music. She moved with him, following his firm lead, thrilling to the touch of his body, the closeness when he executed a complicated step. But a step or two away was the lovely dentist. Joanna said suddenly, 'Can we go home?'

CHAPTER SEVEN

SOME days later, Dan Bruce lingered, chatting to Malika, waiting for Joanna to finish the morning's cases. Joanna had an idea he was there, and was trying to spin out her work as long as possible. She didn't like speaking to Dan in the medical centre. The girls were always on the alert for any gossip, and Joanna didn't want yet another quarrel to be added to the already long list since she arrived to be Dan's locum and dogsbody.

She could hear the voices. She was determined not to leave her room until Dan had left. Dan could have no doubt about her feelings, after that doomed dinner date, when Melanie Ferrara had danced past them, and Joanna knew at last where his loyalty lay. No wonder he had dashed away so readily! Melanie Ferrara worked in Constanza. At last his secret was out.

Finally their voices disappeared, and Malika's cheerful banter ceased. Joanna knew just how much the pretty receptionist appreciated it when her boss found time to stop and chat; Malika always tried to spin out their conversations. Dan must have left, and Malika must be tidying up and filing the patients' records. Joanna left her room and walked along the cool carpeted corridor towards the foyer.

Then she paused. Dan was sitting on Malika's desk with his back to Joanna, leafing through a surgical instrument catalogue. There was no sign of Malika. 'Good afternoon, Joanna.' He didn't turn round. 'You've been a long time.'

'Yes.' She waited for him to turn and look at her before she said weakly, 'I had a few things to—put away.'

'You were hiding.'

'What rubbish. . .' But her voice trailed away. There wasn't much that escaped Dan Bruce's keen blue eyes, and her common sense told her not to try and fool him. Instead she went on the offensive. 'Not in a hurry, Dan? I would have thought your lovely lady friend was waiting impatiently by now. You don't usually keep her waiting.'

He smiled openly, and his eyes crinkled at the corners and looked even more beautiful. He held out a hand, beckoning her to come closer. Joanna took one small step. 'What is it?'

'I wanted to talk to you.'

'Yes—well, if Malika has gone to lunch, I was supposed to be going with her.'

'Joanna, for goodness' sake stop and listen to me! I want your advice. I was thinking we ought to be making use of one of the spare consulting-rooms down the corridor.'

She gave a curt laugh of derision. 'Another doctor? There isn't work for the two of us some days. You have a ridiculously fit lot of patients.' She sauntered closer to him, ready to tease a little. 'Unless, of course, you're thinking of taking even more time off yourself. I wouldn't put that past you.'

He put the catalogue down and caught her arm, forcing her to stand facing him, looking up into his face. A lock of blond hair fell over his forehead, and she yearned to touch it, put it back for him. . . . He said, 'Does the idea of me spending every afternoon in the arms of a lovely woman bother you?'

Her breathing was unsteady as she tried to lie. 'Of course not.'

'Would you like it to be you?' She could feel the warmth of his breath on her cheek.

She shook his hand from her arm, and snapped, 'Don't be utterly crazy!'

Dan said softly, 'Oh, Joanna. . .' Then he took a deep breath and picked up the catalogue again. 'Back to business. I wasn't thinking of another doctor. I thought we should employ a dentist a couple of times a week.'

That figured. She could guess which dentist he had in mind. But she wasn't going to let it appear that she cared one way or the other. 'I suppose it makes sense,' she agreed. 'At present the hotel guests have to go down to Constanza. A session here twice a week—if she can spare the time——'

'What makes you say "she", Joanna?'

'Oh—you know a male dentist as well, do you?'

He laughed. 'It is Señorita Ferrara, actually.'

'What a surprise.'

'Do you mind?'

'Not a bit. I told you, it's an excellent idea.'

'Good. Then maybe you would have a word with her, would you? I have to be off, I'm afraid. She'll be here in a few minutes. Give her lunch, show her round—I'm very grateful, Joanna. Very grateful.' And he threw the catalogue on the desk and made for the door.

'But wait! Just a minute——'

'What is it now? I'm late.'

He had stopped, and returned to stand in front of her. She looked up at him, not knowing what she wanted to say. 'I—don't know—what she'll be paid or anything.'

'Find out which days are suitable. Tell her the hotel will pay her what she asks. OK?'

'Yes.'

'And the catalogue is here. Ask her to choose the equipment she needs.'

'Yes.'

He reached out and took her hand in his. 'What else is wrong?' His voice had sunk to a whisper.

She snatched her hand away. 'Nothing. I guess you're asking me to do it so that no one here will know about your relationship with her.'

Dan's mouth curved as he suppressed a smile, but couldn't hide the amusement in his eyes. 'You could be right. 'Bye, Joanna.'

She watched the door swinging after him, as the infuriating Dr Bruce disappeared into the sunlit gardens. Then she walked back to the desk and sat down, staring into space. Oh, God, Dan, I wish I didn't love you so much. She didn't want to think it, but she knew it was true. She was alive when Dan was there, and only existing when he wasn't. She sighed deeply. Just like a schoolgirl with a crush on a teacher, she thought. Oh, well, I expect it will pass off. Especially as your beautiful dentist will be here, reminding me that I'm too late. Too late, Dan, to make any impression on your heart.

She sat staring at the floor, reminding herself that

it was Roger Fordham whom she really loved, and Roger Fordham she had promised to marry. She was glad now that he was coming for Christmas. They would have a lovely time, and show Dan Bruce quite clearly that she didn't care a rap if he spent over half his days and nights with Melanie Ferrara.

She didn't hear the door swish open. Then suddenly that very English voice crackled through the still air, blotting out the gentle trickle of the fountain. 'Dr Bliss? We met at the Casa Rivero, I think. You're Dan's partner?'

Joanna sprang to her feet, and impulsively held out her hand. 'I'm sorry, I was miles away. Yes, my name is Joanna, and Dr Bruce asked me to make you welcome. Have you had lunch?'

The woman smiled. She had abundant dark hair that fell to just below her shell-like ears, and a shapely, lissom figure with a tiny waist. 'I don't eat lunch, Joanna, but I'll have a mineral water with you while we talk terms.' No lunch—that was obvious. Oh, well, Joanna could manage without as well. She didn't want to feel even more of a rough provincial than she did already.

'We'll go to the golf club,' she suggested. 'Or would you like to look around here first? Dan has left the catalogue for you to choose what you need.'

'I haven't really made my mind up yet,' said Melanie Ferrara. 'Dan only sprang the idea on me last night. To be honest, Joanna, I do like my leisure time. It's too hot on Hernandez to work full-time.'

That figured too. Melanie would want her afternoons off, so that she could spend them in Dan's arms. Joanna said, her voice hardening slightly, 'I take it mornings would suit you better.'

'Oh, mornings, of course. Does anyone work in the afternoons, my dear?' The voice was brittle and patronising.

Joanna showed her round. 'How long have you lived here?' She wasn't really interested, but felt she had to show some manners.

'This is my first job, actually. I trained in London, and I have so many friends there, I'd love to go back. But I expect you can tell by my name that my father was born here, and I had some silly notion that I ought to see his native land before settling down.'

'Hernandez is a beautiful island.'

'Oh, yes. But somehow I hanker after Switzerland.'

Oh, good. Joanna hid a flicker of hope. 'You won't stay here—in Constanza, I mean—for very long, then?'

Melanie laughed. 'There are so many unpredictables in life, aren't there? I would have gone back to the UK by now if I hadn't met a certain young man, who wants to stay here forever.'

Joanna's hopes fell about her in fragments. 'Oh? That doesn't square up with Switzerland.'

'Well, maybe it does. When we're married—or should I say "if"? Then we can work hard here for about eight months, and have a house in Switzerland for the entire winter sports season.'

'Sounds great.'

Melanie's shrill laugh threatened to crack the

glass. 'I'm quite an organiser, Joanna. I like to keep my men on their toes. Are you married?'

'Er—no.' The question was sudden. 'Engaged.'

'Anyone famous?'

Joanna tried to laugh, but the attempt was feeble. 'Not yet—but maybe when his research wins him a Nobel Prize.'

'How interesting.' Melanie sounded extremely bored. 'Right, thanks for showing me round. I'll take the catalogue with me and browse a little. I'll be in touch with Danny, tell him, just as soon as I've made my mind up.'

'OK.' Grateful she didn't have to listen to the empty chatter any longer, Joanna said goodbye politely, and headed for the beach. Malika was sitting at the café, drinking lemonade from a tall frosted glass. 'Just what I need,' said Joanna fervently.

'You look done in. How was Melanie?'

'Dan told you about her?'

'Sure. He may be a strict boss, but he wouldn't do anything behind our backs. It's a good idea, having a dentist.'

'Have you met Melanie Ferrara?'

Malika smiled. 'Of course. She's my dentist—I go to her surgery in Constanza. She's a bit of a society bitch, but she's an excellent dentist, and that's what our guests want, isn't it?'

'I suppose so.' After a long drink of cold lemonade, Joanna cooled down. 'You don't think Dan chose her because she's good to look at?'

Malika giggled. 'Don't you think he gets enough women chasing after him to employ another?

Anyway, in her white coat and glasses, with her hair tied back, she looks like any other female dentist.' Malika looked across with a sly smile. 'Hey, you know? That's what Dr Bruce said you would say!'

Joanna blushed. Dr Bruce had a way of being right that she found extremely annoying. She finished her lemonade, and got her own back by imitating Melanie's artificial accent. 'I don't eat lunch, but I'll sip a mineral water with you!'

'You'd better eat lunch, Joanna. You're on call, and you know what that means.' Malika beckoned the dark-skinned waiter. 'José, the doctor would like beans, rice and *tostónes*.'

'How do you know what I'd like?'

José grinned at her. 'She know what give you much energy, Doctor.'

'Oh, all right, then.'

Later, they swam for a while, and slept under the casuarina trees. The sea glittered as far as the horizon. The shouts of holidaymakers sailing the tiny dinghies, or windsurfing, mingled with the chatter and laughter of children riding ponies, and playing handball or just digging in the sand. It was a good life. Joanna would have been totally contented, but for the niggling fact that she had become quite besotted, along with all the nurses and the receptionists at the medical centre, with Dr Dan Bruce. And she couldn't help wondering where he was now.

'One day, Malika, I'm going to follow Dr Bruce. He's so damn secretive about where he goes.'

Malika lifted herself on an elbow and looked across. 'Don't, Joanna. It's his business.'

'But I do so much extra work for him. I feel I have a right to know why.'

Malika said seriously, 'I don't want you to get hurt.'

'Why should it hurt me?'

'I think you know as well as I do.'

Joanna turned away and lay on her back, closing her eyes so that all she saw of the sun was a red mist. 'I'm not falling for Dan, Malika,' she lied.

'Maybe. Maybe not.'

'My fiancé is coming soon.'

'Sure.'

'Dr Bruce is merely the man I work for. And work damn hard.'

'Yes, Joanna.'

Joanna took a deep breath. After a while she said, 'Does it really show?'

'To me. Maybe no one else realises.'

'I'd better try a bit harder to hide it.'

'You'd better. Especially with your fiancé coming.'

'How?'

Malika tried to be comforting. 'Once you meet your Roger again, you'll soon get over it—realise who you really care for.'

'Yes.'

The pager bleeped. Relieved to have something to do, apart from brood, Joanna pulled her dress on over her swimsuit, and the girls made their way back to the medical centre.

'Telephone for you, Dr Bliss.'

Joanna took it. 'Hello?'

'Hello, Joanna.' There was no mistaking that dark, teasing voice. 'How did it go with Melanie?'

'You haven't seen her?' No, of course, she shouldn't have said that. Blushing, Joanna went on, 'She was going to contact you when she'd thought it over.'

'Did you get the idea she's interested?'

'I think so.'

'Good.' There was a pause, then he said, 'No calls while I was away?'

'Nothing yet.'

'Right.' Another pause. 'Just wanted to make sure you weren't getting up to any mischief.'

She closed her eyes, and tried to control the beating of her heart. 'No.' But then frustration at hearing his voice, and knowing he had rung only because of Melanie, made her burst out, 'It's all right for you to go off and do your own thing! You don't have any right to question me, Dan Bruce! I'm on call, and I'll deal with whatever crops up. I don't need your snide remarks, do you hear?'

'I hear.'

'So what else do you want to know?'

'Nothing. Take it easy, Dr Bliss. I thought you'd be glad I called. You were furious the day you had to do that cholecystectomy, because I hadn't been in touch. Now you're complaining.'

Joanna was annoyed with herself now. 'I'm sorry.'

He said quietly, 'You're sweet,' and rang off.

Angry, but puzzled, she banged the receiver down, before remembering Malika's warning. She had to be much more circumspect about her feelings. It wouldn't do, any more, to fly off the handle, to lash Dan Bruce with her tongue when there were others around. She must try very hard not to care what he got up to. She must try to pretend that his activities didn't matter a jot to her.

It was fortunate she had a tennis game booked with one of the coaches. Hitting that little helpless ball with all her pent-up frustration was a marvellous way of ridding herself of her tension. Joanna changed and strolled along to the courts, just as the sun was setting, and the strip lights were going on around the complex. She paused, seeing her partner hadn't finished the match he was playing, and walked along by the courts, gazing out to sea, to the setting sun, and the wonderful glory of the sunset splayed out across the Caribbean.

'It's beautiful, isn't it?'

She spun round. Dan Bruce stood, in his whites, his racket casually over his shoulder. 'Antonio is busy,' he told her. 'I'll give you a game.'

'How can you possibly spare your valuable time, Dcotor?' Shock brought out her sarcasm again. She had no other defence, no other way of hiding her real feelings of joy at seeing him.

'Do you want to play or don't you?'

'I do.'

'Then let's go.' And they walked along between the courts, finding one free. 'Better spray your arms and legs. Here, let me.' He took the mosquito repellant from his sports bag, and covered her limbs liberally. Then he handed her the can, and she repaid the favour over his tanned muscular arms and legs. 'The little beggars are supercharged at this time of day.'

'I know.'

She took a ball and walked round to the other side of the net. They knocked a few practice balls. Gradually she forgot her emotional plight, and began to enjoy the game. 'Right, Dan, I'll play you a set. And don't go easy on me just because I'm a woman.'

'A woman, are you? I thought you were a dragon, the way you shout at me.'

'Just wait till I start hitting at you!'

He did start by going easy on her, and Joanna took great delight in belting his short strokes into the corners where he couldn't reach them. He soon realised he had to play harder to get the points, and the game became furious. He won the set, but had to fight for every point, and admitted it. 'Give you one more set,' he told her.

'Sure.' The adrenalin of being with him helped her game. She lashed out at every ball, trying, by winning tennis points, to come to terms with his superiority over her in life. They played until the night was dark, and the fireflies danced at the water's edge. Dan won. But he was lavish in praise.

'You're a fighter, Dr Bliss.'

'You already knew that.' Her voice was gentle now. Physical weariness prevented any further verbal sparring between them.

'I'll wait for you.' He stood as she turned into the women's changing-rooms.

'No need.'

He smiled. Joanna showered and changed, combed her damp hair back. It had been an unexpected pleasure, meeting him like that, at a time when usually he was never in the Palacio at all. And the game had been deeply satisfying, being able to hit out at him by proxy, thwack the tennis ball as though it was her own feebleness she was trying to destroy.

'Leave your things in the villa and come dancing with me,' said Dan when she emerged.

He had been waiting, his own fair hair dark with the shower. She said, 'No way, Dan.'

'Why?'

'You know.'

'Roger? He isn't here yet. And your muscles will seize up after that match unless you exercise them gently for a while.'

'That's true,' she admitted. 'I did try very hard to beat you.'

They danced. Too tired to argue with him, she floated in the gentle circle of his arm, feeling the forbidden sweetness of his breath on her cheek, the soft closeness of his face, and the warm desirableness of his body.

They drank Cuba *libre*, and ate titbits of cold pork, sausage, cheese and fresh pineapple. The moon glowed bright and golden behind the trees with their fairy lights and nightingales. Joanna wished the world would end just then. It was so perfect, without having to think of Roger, or of Melanie Ferrara. They were together, talking quietly, with no acrimony, no need for rudeness or sarcasm. Occasionally Dan reached out his hand to touch her cheek, in an intimate gesture of spontaneous closeness.

He walked back to the villa with her, side by side,

but not touching. At the door, he drew her close, kissed her briefly on the forehead. 'Can we do this again?' he asked softly.

'I'd like to.'

She watched him walk away, between the hibiscus bushes. He turned once, and lifted his hand in farewell. Joanna opened the door at last and let herself in. She leaned against the door, shaking her head in self-pity. Oh, Roger, what am I going to do? I can't help it. I can't stop it. I'm just hopelessly, endlessly. . . And he isn't mine to claim. And I'm not his.

CHAPTER EIGHT

DR BRUCE, however, didn't ask her again for a
while. Their work at the medical centre was unevent-
ful, and he continued with his urgent departures,
after only a word or two after the morning sessions.
He remained behind twice, when there was minor
surgery to carry out. Then they worked closely, and
he complimented Joanna on her growing operational
confidence. Now and again she caught him looking
at her, his blue eyes thoughtful. But he said nothing
beyond the normal bounds of daily politeness and
necessity. Joanna held in her feelings. It was perhaps
all for the best.

And then Roger arrived. He had written that he
would telephone her from Miami, so Joanna continued her usual routine, eating fruit with Malika at
lunchtime, and having a swim. She would eat in any
of the restaurants at night, sometimes alone, sometimes with the tennis coach, and occasionally with
Malika and Valentino. It was the night Valentino
brought along Fidel, one of the polo players, to
make up a four for dancing, that Roger appeared.

It was all quite innocent. Joanna was dancing with
Fidel, who was black, lithe, and an excellent dancer.
They were at the open-air dance-floor, which had no
walls, and just a thatched roof above them. The
orchestra were dressed in frilled scarlet shirts, and
the blue of the floodlit swimming pool made a

colourful background. The music pulsed excitingly, and they danced with vigour and style, now that she had been here long enough to learn the steps well, to understand how to sublimate herself to the rhythm of the music, and respond to the skilled guidance of her partner.

It was Malika who put her hand on Fidel's shoulder to get them to notice her. 'Sorry to butt in, but there's a man looking at you, Joanna.'

Fidel smiled and said, 'She ain't available.'

But Joanna had sensed urgency in Malika's voice. She knew who it was before she caught sight of him—a slim, nervous white-skinned figure among all the suntans and the dark beauties in vivid clothes. 'It's my fiancé!' Joanna exclaimed. 'It's Roger!'

Malika said, 'You go. I'll explain.'

Fidel said, 'No need. I know what a fiancé is, Joanna.'

'I'm sorry to break up the party.'

'No problem. *Hasta luego*, partner.'

Joanna shook back her hair. She had allowed it to grow long, and it curled about her head on to her shoulders, its usual light brown burnt blonder by the sun. She walked to Roger, and looked up into his face, saw his eyes flicker to Fidel and back, and his mouth tighten. 'I wasn't expecting you, Roger,' she said.

'I see that. I couldn't get through when I tried to ring from Miami. And I had to run for the connection.' He put down his travel bag and wiped his forehead with a handkerchief. Then he leaned towards her, and kissed her cheek. 'Good to see you, Jo.'

'You too.' She wasn't sure what to say. 'Would you like a drink? I haven't booked you in at the hotel.'

'I'd love a beer. And do you need to book me in? I thought you said you have your own villa.'

'Yes. Yes, I have. But it's—on the small side.'

'We have shared smallish bedrooms in our time.' His look was keen, and Joanna blushed. 'Knowing your passionate nature, I expected a bit of a warmer welcome than that.'

Joanna hastily led him away, found another café where the atmosphere was less vibrantly sensual. 'Would you like to taste Hernandean rum?'

'Just beer, please.' She ordered beer, and a Cuba *libre* for herself. He said, 'Who was that man you were dancing with?'

'He's a professional polo player—very good, actually. I don't know him very well. He's Malika's friend—she's the girl I was with. I'll introduce you properly tomorrow.'

Roger drained his glass. 'God, it's hot! How you can dance like that in this heat!'

'I'm acclimatised now,' Joanna explained. 'You'll soon be more comfortable. I'll take you to the beach tomorrow.'

He accepted a second beer. 'And you're still enjoying the work?'

'Oh, yes.'

'Boss OK?'

'Yes, he's OK. Not around much, actually.'

Roger looked at her in the candlelight. 'You look extraordinarily well, Jo. It obviously suits you here.'

'I love it.'

'Yes—I loved the Himalayas, but I was glad to get home.'

'How's the research?'

'Pretty good, thanks. I've published a preliminary paper in the *BMJ*.'

'That's great.'

They were speaking like acquaintances only. Then Roger said, 'As I was saying—your passionate nature—it occurred to me that you might be missing that side of our life.'

Joanna drew herself up. 'I resent that implication, Roger. I made you a promise, and I haven't broken it.'

'I'm sorry, old thing. I didn't mean—well, maybe I meant I've been missing you.'

'It's all right.' But it wasn't. Because Roger was wanting to stay in the villa, and Joanna didn't want him there, sleeping in her bedroom, assuming he had some sort of right over her. 'I've got used to living alone,' she explained. 'That's why I think you should stay at the hotel. We aren't married, Roger— and I don't know if you realise, this is a very strict Catholic country. I don't want people talking about me.'

'Very well, I'll take a room. But we can spend the days together, I hope?'

'Of course we can.'

She led the way to the main hotel block, greeting people she knew on the way, introducing Roger to the staff, the managers, the golf pros. 'You certainly are popular, Joanna.'

'It's a close community.' There was a suite available on the top floor. Joanna took Roger to the lift.

As the doors swung open, Dan Bruce stepped out, immaculate in a dark dinner-jacket and black tie, his glossy hair tamed into a neat style, but still eye-catching in the light.

'Hey, Joanna—what are you doing here?' His smile was welcoming. 'Shall we——?' But he stopped, realising in time that she wasn't alone. 'I'm sorry.'

'This is Roger Fordham, Dan. Roger, this is Dan Bruce.'

The two men shook hands. Roger said, 'Don't mind me. Ask Jo what you were going to.' His voice was cool, his eyes cooler.

It was very obvious that Joanna was working with one of the best-looking men in the Palacio, if not in Constanza. It was also obvious that she had never mentioned Dan's looks, or his comparative youth, leading Roger to expect an older man, and certainly one with no charisma. Roger looked from one to the other with pointed irony. Dan said cheerfully, 'Only going to offer her a cup of tea, Dr Fordham. No problem. Nice meeting you. You must come along and look round the medical centre tomorrow—I look forward to seeing you. Goodnight.'

Roger said nothing until they were inside the hotel room. Then he put his bag down and turned to Joanna with hostile eyes. 'I'm sorry, Joanna, I thought I'd be welcome here. But first I find I'm not to stay with you, and now I find your boss to be a highly eligible dandy. You should have told me I'd be spoiling your fun!'

She looked at him pleadingly. 'Roger, please don't jump to conclusions. Yes, Dan is good-looking. He's also heavily involved with a very glamorous dentist. He takes a lot of time off, which infuriates me because I have to work unexpected hours, and I've already had about three blazing rows with your "eligible dandy". There's absolutely nothing between us.'

'Nothing of a sexual nature, you mean?'

'Nothing of any nature,' snapped Joanna. 'For goodness' sake, Roger, grow up! I work with the man. You work with women, don't you? That's all. Full stop.'

He took a deep breath. 'I haven't spoiled anything?'

'No.'

'And you're glad to see me?'

'Very glad. Very happy that you went to all this expense to make our Christmas a happy one together.'

Roger's face finally softened. 'Come here, Jo.' His drawn, dark-rimmed eyes and grey skin told of his jet-lag, but his embrace was strong, and his kisses searching. He had missed her. She hadn't thought he would. She had never thought his physical need was quite so pressing. When he dragged the neckline of her dress down, tearing off two buttons, kissing her neck and breast with increasing violence, forcing her down on to the bed, Joanna wondered if this could be the same Roger whom she had to tease away from his books sometimes. And she knew she didn't want his intimacy. Not like this. She had quite simply fallen out of love. And therefore these urgent attentions amounted to rape, because she was unwilling, and his efforts to arouse her brought only distaste.

His hands covered, squeezed and kneaded her body roughly, and his touch gave no pleasure. In a moment she would have to say so, and any further engagement, any commitment, would have to be terminated. Out of pity, out of the memory of what they used to mean to each other, Joanna didn't want it to be like that. Yet as she turned her head away, avoiding his seeking mouth, she knew this couldn't go on. She was taking a breath, preparing to speak, when the pager bleeped. Roger sat up, enquiring. Joanna sagged on to the bed, never more delighted to hear that urgent little summons.

'I have to go, Roger.'

'So I see.' His breathing was heavy, his eyes half closed with desire. 'Want me to——?'

'You're exhausted with jet-lag, darling. Get some sleep. I'll be at the medical centre tomorrow. I'll wait for you. Goodnight, Roger.'

She escaped, blessing the patient who needed her at such an opportune moment. But as she walked over the gardens, pulling her dress around her neck, hoping no one would notice the missing buttons, she felt sad, because she would have to tell Roger she couldn't love him any more.

The medical centre was in darkness at the front. Only the hospital rooms were lit, the night nurses on duty. Joanna paused at the door, not bothering to go in. Maybe the pager had gone off by accident. But then she saw someone coming towards her, and recognised the dapper figure of her boss. 'Did you page me, Dan?' she asked.

He came up to her, and nodded. 'Sorry. It was tactless, to say the least. I wasn't sure—if you wanted to stay there or not. I got the impression when I met you by the lift that you weren't getting on all that well with each other.'

'So you bleeped me! And what do I say when Roger asks me who the patient was?'

'Are you annoyed?'

'You've got a real cheek, Dr Bruce, sir!'

'Then why are you smiling?'

'I'm not smiling!' She didn't think he could see her in the darkness. When he suddenly bent and found her lips with his, it was pure joy to be kissed when she wanted to kiss back. 'I must go, though.'

His hand brushed against her dress, and in the starlight, he saw the neckline gaping open. 'Oh, Joanna!' he muttered.

She clutched the edges together. 'He was a bit over-excited. Goodnight, Dan.'

She knew he was watching her go. She knew he wanted to see if she went home, or back to Roger. She went home, locked herself in, and flung herself naked on the bed in the heat of the night. Men! How much less hassle to sleep alone. Yet as she tossed and turned under the single thin sheet, she knew there was one hard, suntanned body she would have been glad to share it with. Unfortunately, he was unavailable for permanent commitment.

He was already at work when she arrived next morning. Joanna greeted Malika, who said, 'Where is your boyfriend?'

Joanna said demurely, 'I found him a room at the hotel.'

Malika shrieked with laughter. 'Oh, Joanna, how could you? Did he ask about Fidel?'

'He did. And about Dr Bruce, whom we ran into in the hotel.'

Malika's amusement quietened. 'You met Dr Bruce?'

'Yes. I introduced them. Roger may come along later, if he wakes up in time.'

'But, Joanna, what are you going to do?'

'There's very little I can do. I'll be in my room if any patients turn up, Malika.'

'Yes, Doctor.' Malika's tone was sympathetic. But Joanna was right. There was nothing anyone could do, except take each moment as it came.

A few patients came for minor consultations, and Joanna was glad to be kept occupied. But the prospect of entertaining Roger, while at the same time keeping him at bay, was puzzling and worrying her. In the end, she would have to tell him the truth—that her love had cooled, that it had never really been the kind of love that settled down into a loving marriage. It would spoil his Christmas—and hers. But it was the only honest thing to do.

It was almost midday. Joanna looked at her watch. Time to pack up and go in search of lunch—and in her case, Roger as well. There was a sudden tap at the door. 'Come in,' she called.

It was Roger. He looked as though he hadn't slept very well. She looked at his pale, uninteresting face, and wished he hadn't taken the trouble to fly all the way here. Yet maybe it was good in a way—because it had brought things to a head. She knew now how little she loved him. If he had stayed away, she might have gone on thinking that her lack of passion towards him was only because he was a long way away. 'Hello, Jo. Am I welcome?' he asked.

The words cut her heart. He sounded as though he already knew what she was going to say. 'Of course, darling.' She rose and went to him, forced herself to reach up and kiss his cheek. How lifeless his skin was to her lips. 'I think we're finished here. Shall I show you around?'

'Yes, thanks. Your boss here?'

'I expect he's in his room. He might have a patient. We won't bother him.'

But Dan came through at that moment. 'Good morning, Dr Fordham—glad you could come. I have to dash, but feel free to wander around. By the way, Joanna, I had a call from Melanie, and she's willing to start after Christmas.'

'Oh, fine. That gives us time to install the dentist's chair and the other torture instruments.'

Dan laughed. 'You can't say that about Melanie. She's the gentlest dentist in the business. Ask anyone.'

'I believe you.'

Dan waved his hand in general farewell. Joanna turned away quickly, remembering and trying not to enjoy the thought of that snatched kiss last night. 'Come on, Roger. You've seen my room. I'll take you along to the hospital wing. We have about three in-patients at the moment.'

'Get any children?'

'Hardly any. We had one appendicitis last month, a couple of jellyfish stings. None of what you would call problems.'

They walked around. Joanna found herself lingering, in an attempt to keep Roger occupied, postponing the moment when they would have to be together. He asked, 'Where do you usually go for lunch?'

'Quite often I go with Malika to the beach café.'

'Sounds fun. I wouldn't mind being on call if I could lounge on a beach.'

'Want to go?'

'Yes, please.'

'Then go and put your swimming trunks on under your trousers. We can hire towels and sun-loungers.'

'You mean you come to work already wearing a swimsuit?'

'Yes, I do. And just about everyone else around here.'

While Roger went away to do as he was told, Joanna put her hand to her forehead, wishing she knew what she could do to make things a little easier.

Malika said, 'Dr Bruce is on call. He took the pager, Joanna, otherwise I could call you back a couple of times.'

Joanna composed her face and looked steadily at the pretty receptionist. 'What makes you think I want to be called away?'

'Instinct,' Malika smiled, and Joanna had to give in and grin ruefully back. Malika said, 'I could take him out for a sail?'

Joanna's eyes widened with relief. 'I say, yes—please do that if you don't mind. He enjoys sailing, and I never have.'

'Just not suited, are you, Doctor?' asked Malika archly.

Joanna shook her head. 'But I just never realised. We had some good times together.'

'You said it was his idea to broaden your mind by travel.'

'Yes, it was. I didn't even think of working abroad. I was all set to finish my GP training and look for a suitable assistantship.'

Malika said thoughtfully, 'Do you think he realised that?'

'Realised what?'

'That you had led a very narrow life? Maybe he knew you weren't ready to settle down really.'

'I would have settled down quite happily if I hadn't come here and met——' Joanna was speaking loudly, protesting, when she saw Roger approaching, and her torrent of words suddenly dried up. 'Hi, Roger.'

Roger came in, nodding affably at Malika. 'I hear you usually have lunch together. Don't let me be a drag. Come with us. You can tell me what Jo's really like as a boss.' There was a hint of a twinkle in his grey eyes.

Malika responded to his generosity. 'Not today, Doctor. Maybe when you've been here a couple of days, I'll join you. But you must have a lot to talk about.'

'That's very thoughtful of you.'

'Not a bit. I do have some unfinished business to attend to over at the polo field.'

Roger smiled at her. 'That would be Fidel? The young man I saw?'

'The other one, Doctor. Fancy you noticing!'

'You made a handsome couple,' was the gallant reply, as Joanna led him off towards the beach.

Roger seemed much more relaxed, as they walked across the grass, alongside the golf course, towards the beach. They could just see the masts of the windsurfers above the trees, and hear the shouts of the children swimming, and the radios playing local dance music. He said, 'I'm not surprised your boss was in such a hurry to get away.' He sounded ever so slightly smug.

'Why? Did you see him?'

'I did indeed. He was kissing a very beautiful brunette.'

Joanna stifled pangs of jealousy. 'That would be Melanie. I'm afraid she does get a lot more of his time than his patients do.'

'Well, I'm very sorry I doubted you. Blame my jet-lag. Anyone who has a woman like that——'

'Wouldn't look at a woman like me?' Joanna was exploiting Roger's obvious admiration for Melanie. It made her own position so much more safe, if Roger believed her to be no competition for Melanie. Not that she was any competition whatsoever. But she knew she had more of Dan's attention than Roger now believed, and the sight of the lovely dentist had done Joanna a favour.

'I didn't mean that,' he said. 'You're a lovely woman, Jo.'

'I didn't come here to be a lovely woman. I came to be a doctor, and that's what I'm doing.'

Roger put his arm round her. 'And thank goodness you haven't got that blessed bleep in your handbag this afternoon. We can have the afternoon to ourselves, love. I want to get to know you all over again.'

They lay in the half-shadow under the trees, not wanting Roger to burn in the hot sun. Joanna kept thinking of Dan kissing Melanie in full view of Roger, and presumably everyone passing by. 'Where was it you saw Dan and Melanie, Roger?' she asked.

'Right outside the hotel.'

'And they were kissing?'

'He was kissing her.'

'On the lips?'

'On the cheek. But it was pretty hot stuff.'

Joanna closed her eyes. It was probably just the traditional greeting. Dan wouldn't parade his lady-love like that. Not after all the trouble he went to, to keep his afternoon trysts a secret from his staff. Roger had misinterpreted what he had seen. But let him go on thinking. It was, after all, the truth.

Roger had suddenly got up and pulled his lounger close against Joanna's. 'Not jealous of her, Jo?'

'Not jealous one iota.' She raised herself on an elbow to look down at him. 'Can't you see, Roger? He's one of those men who use their good looks to get them their own way. He's a very selfish person, and it didn't take me long to find that out.'

'But you like him?'

'He has a cheerful nature. But we don't get on. I shout at him too much.'

'He can't enjoy that. Good for you, Jo.'

'That's what I thought.'

They lay for a while, almost asleep, listening to the sound of the waves, the oaths of the windsurfer who kept falling off, and the laughter of his mates. But then Roger's arm crept over her waist. His fingers caressed her skin, sliding underneath the bikini top and encasing her breast with a sticky palm. 'You're lovely, Jo. Suntan suits you. And you have more life about you.'

'Not at the moment, Roger—I'm sleepy. Let me have half an hour?'

His fingers kneaded the breast, played with the nipple. At one time it would have given her a thrill of stimulation, roused her from her torpor. But now it disgusted her, and she tensed her body, trying not to wince at his familiarity. How did she tell him that she had changed? That she didn't see him as a lover, but only as a friend? She drew in her breath to tell him to stop. At that moment they heard someone calling her name. Roger's arm was replaced at his side in a second, and Joanna was able to replace her bra top where it belonged. She rolled over on to her stomach. She mustn't give him such an opportunity again.

'Hi, Joanna.' Malika came up, innocently bright, dressed in shorts and a T-shirt. 'Hi, Dr Fordham.'

'You can call me Roger.' He sat up, leaned on an elbow, pretending to have just woken up.

'I'm going sailing,' said Malika. 'Want to come?'

'Love to. Wouldn't we, Jo?' Roger had been eyeing the little boats. Perfect weather for it, with the warm sun, and a decent breeze. He scrambled from his recumbent position. It was too late to change his mind, when Joanna refused.

'I'm just so tired, Malika,' she explained.

'Come on, Roger; let's see how you handle a real Hernandean wind,' challenged Malika.

'OK, then. See you in a while, Jo, love.'

'Right. Enjoy yourselves,' Joanna said sleepily. But she was awake enough to exchange a wink with Malika, as her friend ran off after Roger.

CHAPTER NINE

CHRISTMAS EVE came round. Roger had begun to realise that Joanna didn't welcome physical contact as much as he had hoped. But they went out a lot, swam, danced, and went to concerts and films. It was lucky that it was the festive season, as the hotel was swarming with musicians, with Hollywood stars, and famous polo players. A couple of the world's top tennis players came to give an exhibition, and a leading footballer entered the golf tournament. There was never a moment when nothing was going on, and hence very few occasions when they were alone together.

'What shall we do on Christmas Eve?' he asked her.

'Christmas Eve is the family day, Roger. They have their turkey then, and give their presents, so that Christmas Day itself can be spent on the beach after church.'

'It seems very odd, having turkey in this heat.'

'We don't need to. We can eat anything we want. We're on holiday.'

They were sitting by the tennis courts, eating ice-cream, and hoping for a glimpse of the great Kaminsky practising. Roger said, 'To be honest, Jo, I'd intended to buy you an engagement ring for Christmas. We never bought one in Moreton. I

126

thought it would be nice to get it here, in Constanza—to remind you of Hernandez, when we sit at home by the fire. Would you like that?'

'Hello there, Roger, Joanna.' Dan Bruce came over, kitted out in whites. 'Want a knock-up?'

Joanna said, trying not to look glad to see him, 'What are you doing here at this time?'

'I, Dr Bliss, have been asked to give the great Stefan Kaminsky a work-out. And I thought you might like to join us. How about you, Roger? The three of us could maybe give him a decent game?'

Roger said, slightly annoyed at the interruption, 'I don't play to any standard. Neither does Jo.'

'That's where you're wrong,' Dan told him. 'She's been training with one of our best coaches. How about it, Joanna?'

'I'd be thrilled to play against Kaminsky, if he doesn't mind.'

'I told him I could probably find someone to test him out! Go and get changed.'

Dan sat by Roger, chatting cheerfully, until Joanna came back. Then he stood up and led the way to the court. Kaminsky wasn't there yet. Dan put his hand on her shoulder. 'How's it going?'

If only she could tell him. But he had his life, and she had hers, and there was no point in involving him in her problems. 'No problem, Dan.'

He looked into her eyes. 'You said that like a Hernandean, *querida*. Now, get out there, and let's show this mid-European how to play tennis!'

Joanna was laughing, but her heart had given a sudden lurch when he called her darling. *Querida*. It meant nothing to him. But it gave her a lift, just as it had when he called her *princesa*, only better. 'On guard, then. Here it comes!' And she sent a stinging service skimming over the net. She heard Dan curse as he missed it, and Roger shout encouragement. Then the athletic young tennis star himself came out on to the court, clapping.

'That was very good, *señorita*.' They stopped and introduced themselves. Joanna joined Dan opposite to Kaminsky, and they provided whatever opposition he needed, either smashes, volleys, lobs or services. Dan muttered, as he ran himself out of breath, 'I'm glad you're on my side today. You're in lethal form.'

'It's nothing personal,' she said, reaching for another cruelly low back spin forehand from the young champion, and just getting it back with a grunt.

Eventually the other professional player, a lean American called Dude Danvers, came on to the court, and Kaminsky thanked Dan and Joanna, shook hands with them, and hoped to catch up with them later. Dan said, smiling, 'You'll hope not to, I guess. We're the medicos around here. You'll only see us if you don't want to!'

They went back, after showering and changing, to where Roger had been sitting. There was no sign of him. Joanna looked up at Dan. 'He must have gone back to the hotel,' she decided.

Dan said, 'Then what say we do what we did last time, and go dancing?'

'You're joking, of course.'

'No. I enjoyed it a lot last time. I was going to ask you both. If he isn't here, what can I do about it?'

She found herself in the middle of a deep sigh, and suddenly checked herself. It wasn't right to speak to Dan like this, to let him see her feelings. 'Thanks anyway. But I'll be seeing you around.'

'I'm—on my own tonight. If you change your mind, I'll be at Geraldi's, feeling sorry for myself.'

'What about the million beautiful women?'

He grinned. 'I might look one of them up.'

'You do that, Dan.'

'But see you at the beach tomorrow?'

'Sure. Looking forward to it. We're bringing the salad.'

'And a bottle of rum, don't forget!'

'Goodnight, Dan. Happy Christmas.'

He paused and looked back. She was still looking after him, and their eyes met. He took a step back towards her. It was dusk, and the lights were twinkling in the trees, and the fireflies down among the trees. The atmosphere was electric with expectation, as the restaurants were smartened up for the evening, musicians practised, stages erected, and chefs began the night's feast. 'On my own tonight.' If ever there was a night made just for them, it was now, just beginning.

He had come back to just within earshot. 'Will you?'

Joanna shook her head. 'I can't.'

'You'll never see another Christmas on Hernandez.'

'I will. Some day I will, I know it.' And she turned and walked slowly towards the hotel, towards Roger, dragging her feet, and not with weariness from the tennis.

Roger wasn't in his room. Alarmed, she ran to the villa. He wasn't there either. He was playing some trick. She hoped he hadn't gone to town for an engagement ring—it was just the sort of crazy thing he might do. Joanna went through to the bedroom, and changed slowly into her best green and blue dress. She curled her hair, pinned in some long sparkling earrings. 'But where do I go without Roger? Do I sit here all night?' She dabbed some perfume behind her ears, and between her breasts. She poured herself a Cuba *libre*, mixing just the right amount of lime, as Dan had showed her. The ice clinked, and the crickets sang in the garden. There was a distant sound of carols, drifting through the bright trees. Joanna went outside. How could she miss Christmas Eve, just because Roger had decided to sulk?

Dan was waiting at Geraldi's. He was in dinner-jacket, and looked very handsome, his wild hair tamed a little, his blue eyes the way she liked them, serious and a little sad. He stood up as she came in. It was nearly ten. 'He didn't show?' he asked.

'No.'

'Want to dance? Or eat?'

'Dance.' They went into one another's arms and danced to the slow, rhythmic *salsa*, moving as one person, their bodies sensing each other's movements.

'You think he'll come?'

'I wish I knew.'

'Are you sad?'

'Sad for him. I didn't want him to be unhappy.'

Dan's arms tightened around her, and he danced

with his cheek against hers. To an onlooker, they must have looked the perfect couple. She said softly, 'Where's your date tonight?'

'Busy.'

'Is that all you're going to tell me?'

'It's all there is to tell.' There came a single clear sound of a bell tolling through the music. He said, 'Shall we go to the church? It's beautiful.'

'Yes.'

There was quite a crowd making for the stone chapel in one part of the hotel grounds. Its doors were wide open, and a single choirboy was singing inside, accompanied by a guitar. A priest was there, saying Mass for those who believed. Many were there just for the beauty and the atmosphere. The music swelled, and the congregation joined in, so that their celebration filled the entire complex, reaching down to the golf course and up to the servants' quarters. Joanna felt tears in her eyes. This time next year it would be like this, but she wouldn't be here to join in.

Later they strolled back to Geraldi's and danced again. They said very little, but somehow there was no need. At about two, Joanna said, 'I'll go back now.'

'No need. No work tomorrow.'

'I know.'

Dan didn't argue with her, but walked with his arm gently round her waist. He didn't kiss her at the door. They both knew that somewhere Roger must be watching them. 'Goodnight, Joanna,' he said softly.

'Goodnight.'

Dan stood for a while, looking into her eyes, and she didn't want to go in and have such a beautiful day come to an end. It was Dan who finally looked away, swung on his heel. She watched him stride away, his shoulders erect, his head proud and handsome, like a lion.

She woke next morning with a deep sense of loss. And she knew she hadn't wanted him to leave her alone last night. Still, it was a beautiful morning, bright, with the wisps of morning mist drifting away across the sparkling water. Rosita had left the salad in the fridge. All Joanna had to do was toss it in dressing, and carry the container down to the beach, together with a bottle of rum and an ice-box. She stood in the hall looking at the telephone. Was Roger going to show up?

She was just reaching for the phone to call his room, when the doorbell rang. Roger stood there, in white shorts and a bright short-sleeved shirt, a bottle of wine in each hand. He was smiling broadly, as though nothing had happened. 'Happy Christmas, Jo, dear.'

'Happy Christmas.' She put her arms round his neck and kissed his cheek. 'I was worried!'

'No more of that!' he replied briskly. 'We're going to enjoy ourselves, aren't we?'

'Oh, yes.' Thankfully she collected her things, and they strolled down to the shore. Music already came from transistor radios, and some couples were dancing in the sand, dressed in shorts and sunhats draped with tinsel. Joanna watched Roger, but he seemed quite at ease, as he greeted Malika and Juanita with a resounding kiss on each cheek, and was one of the first to throw off his shorts and shirt and run into the turquoise water for a swim, scattering a family of pelicans who had been sitting serenely on the rocks.

'What's happened to Dr Bruce?' asked Malika.

Joanna said tartly, 'Why are you asking me, Malika? I don't know any more about him that you do.'

'I saw you with him last night. It didn't look as though you were strangers.'

Joanna realised that quite a few people might have seen them last night. She had been so wrapped up in her own feelings, in the warmth and intimacy of Dan's closeness, that she hadn't given much thought to what it had looked like to onlookers. But yes, they had danced closely, and held each other tight for a long time. But it was only as friends, whatever Malika might think. 'Just good friends,' she said tamely, and her explanation was greeted with a round of cynical applause by Juanita.

'Is that for me, or are you being sarcastic?' Dan was running lightly across the sand, carrying a plastic bag. The receptionists and some of the nurses jumped up to give him his Christmas kiss, and he dutifully kissed them soundly on the cheek, and gave them a hug, which Malika said they all looked forward to every year. He handed the bag over. 'Firelighters for the charcoal. And there's some rum in there too.'

Juanita had carried a whole crate of Coca-Cola cans down from their beach buggy to where the barbecue was set up. The nurses whose turn it was to do the cooking were already busy with a trestle table, and Joanna went over to put her salads there, and give a hand opening some of the Coke bottles.

Dan came over to Joanna. 'Happy Christmas.' She looked up from her salad with a smile, and he put his arm round her waist and kissed her on the lips. There was another burst of applause from the girls, and Dan grinned. 'They were watching us.'

'Happy Christmas, Dan.'

'Where's Roger?'

'Swimming already.'

'Think I'd better go and join him. These girls won't leave us alone today, I can tell.' He swept his T-shirt over his head, dishevelling his already untidy mane, and stepped out of his trousers. The girls whistled at him, and he turned back to say to Joanna, 'They know they can be impertinent today. But tomorrow they toe the line again or else!' She smiled, and thought of the day she had met him, when his broad body was twisted round, as it was now, showing off the muscles, the fitness, the sun-tanned skin. She had admired him then, with his piercing eyes the colour of the sky, and his white hair against the background of palm trees. Now it was much more than admiration—so very much more. Joanna turned away.

The savoury smell of home-made burgers began to drift with the blue smoke between the trees. Plastic cups of rum were passed round, and soon everyone was sitting in a group, eating the best Christmas lunch Joanna could remember. Roger sat beside her, totally contented, joking with the girls, and drinking Cuba *libres* until the ice ran out.

Later, they lay in the sun side by side. 'I'll be going tomorrow, Jo,' Roger reminded her.

'Why so soon?'

'Didn't I tell you? I'm in charge of the mess dinner on New Year's Eve, and I haven't even bought the wine yet.'

'The junior doctors' association?'

'That's right.'

'I see.'

He rolled over on his side. 'I had to go soon, anyway. But seeing you last night suddenly showed me I was wasting my time.'

'I only met Dan because you didn't show up.'

'But you wanted to. It didn't need a genius to see what there is between you. Oh, I know he has a girl—and a very pretty one. But I've seen him with Melanie—and I saw him last night with you. And there's just no competition. I don't like to admit it, Jo. He's crazy about you. And you seemed quite agreeable.'

Joanna said, 'I think you're reading things into our relationship that aren't there.'

Roger smiled, his eyes wise. 'I certainly see now why you didn't want me to stay at the villa with you.'

She said quickly, 'Roger, I told you——!'

'I know, I know—nothing physical between you. I believe you. But there soon will be.'

She said testily, 'Can't you tell the difference between a man who cares, and a man who was just lonely that night? His girl was busy, that's all. You went AWOL. We consoled each other!'

Roger said, 'I didn't mention it, Jo—but there's a night sister on Neuro, in Moreton—she makes me coffee from time to time. She's nice. Likes badminton. I thought you'd like to know I haven't been living like a monk.'

Joanna paused, then saw what he was trying to say, smiled at him and reached out to put her hand on his. 'Thanks for telling me.'

And then Dan Bruce came running up from the sea, his hair dripping. 'I'm afraid I have to be going,' he said.

The girls protested, some pretending to cry, some whooping about the girl he was leaving them to meet. Laughing, he pulled on his clothes over his wet things, slipped his feet into his espadrilles, and waved to them all. 'Have a good day.'

Roger got up. 'And I'll say goodbye and good luck, Dan.'

Dan shook his hand firmly. 'Happy New Year, old man.' The two men looked at each other openly, and nodded with what looked like a genuine liking for each other.

Roger said, 'I won't be back.'

Dan said, 'You'd be welcome if you came.'

'Thanks. As I said, good luck.' Roger lifted a hand in farewell, as Dan made his way back to the hotel.

Malika said, 'It would be nice if he'd stay—just once, till the end. We always stay to watch the sunset. You'll stay, won't you, Joanna? And Roger?'

Roger agreed immediately. 'Why not? Can't leave you without any masculine protection.' And Malika laughed, and pulled him up to dance with her. Joanna watched, glad that Roger wasn't too heartbroken. Maybe that night sister helped. . .

Then her hand was taken, and she looked up into the lean dark face of the handsome Valentino. 'Can we join your party?' he asked. He was with about five other boys from the sports centre.

'You certainly can!' The nurses cheered as the boys descended with cans of beer and Coke. Joanna danced with Valentino, but, halfway through the dance, changed partners with Malika, and ended in Roger's arms.

He kissed her, very soundly and very lovingly, and she knew it was a goodbye. 'I hope you'll be happy, Jo. And look me up if you're ever back in Moreton. We'll always be friends, huh?'

'I'll feel quite lonely after you've gone.'

Roger waved his arm at all the beauty around them. 'It's not a bad place to be lonely in.'

'You're right. To think that it was you who persuaded me to work abroad!'

'It's for the best, Jo. You always had a restless streak in you. You thought you were ready to settle down, but I had a feeling you weren't.'

They watched the sunset. It flamed magnificently, then slowly died, leaving tongues of yellow and pink across the calm waters of the bay, dotted with idle fishing boats. Roger and Joanna walked back later, after eating lobster with the others in a rickety seaside café. 'What a finale!' Roger sighed. And she knew he didn't mean just the day, but a finale to their affair.

It was after ten, and she was tired. Roger kissed her once more, but they said no more; it had all been said. Joanna went inside, and closed the door. Roger had said that Dan cared for her—that he could tell from the way they had danced the previous night. But Joanna somehow knew differently. Dan had been attentive recently—but one only had to see the way he had rushed away, still dripping from his swim, in order not to be late for his assignment with Melanie. That was his preoccupation, not being nice to Joanna. She had to tell herself that, and not dream dreams that had no foundation in fact.

The telephone rang, and she picked it up, wondering who would want her on a day when the hospital was manned by locum doctors. It was the night sister. 'Dr Jamis is on his way,' she said. 'I know you aren't on call, but I've tried to get Dr Bruce, and he is incommunicado.'

'What is it? An emergency?'

'I'm afraid so—this young girl that he admitted two days ago. She had an appendicectomy a couple of months ago, and she's got terrible tummy pains again.'

'Under the diaphragm?'

'Yes.'

'Subphrenic abscess?'

'That's what the young locum thinks. Can you do it, Doctor?'

'Yes, I've done this before. It's just a question of how far the infection might have spread internally. I'll come at once.' She brushed as much sand out of her hair as possible, and put on a clean dress. It was annoying, to have to do one of Dan's cases. If he had admitted that girl, he should have borne in mind that she might need further surgery, and made sure the hospital had his telephone number. This was the second time he had done this. She really ought to demand Melanie's home phone number. It was unfair for Dan to be unobtainable.

She arrived within a few minutes. Dr Jamis was already changing. 'I hope you have plenty of local antibiotics?' she said, as she hurried through to the changing-rooms.

'Yes, Doctor. We're well stocked.'

Joanna went through to examine the patient. Yes, under the suntan there was a definite pallor, and under the diaphragm she was very painful. Tears slipped from her eyes, though she was too weak to cry properly. Joanna said, 'Please God we're in time—she looks bad. Get her to theatre at once.'

It was a bad case. The abscess was grossly swollen. It would need delicate skill to remove without spreading any further infection. Joanna pulled her gloves tighter by pressing her fingers together. 'Ready, Dr Jamis?' and at his nod she held out her hand for the scalpel.

She couldn't have done it so successfully without the help of the junior doctor, who, with the sister, kept her supplied with suction, and with swabs. Joanna toiled for an hour, desperate to ensure that not a trace of infection was left inside. 'Blood-pressure low, Joanna.' Dr Jamis was watching the monitor.

'Right—that's it. Antibiotics, please.' She saturated the area, before resuturing the peritoneum, then drawing the skin back, and using the smallest possible stitches to make the wound safe, bearing in mind that if the girl wanted to wear a bikini the neatness of the scar would matter. 'I'll stay around until her BP is normal. Give her packed cells first, and when she responds, a normal plasma.'

The girl regained consciousness. Joanna went home. It was three o'clock in the morning.

CHAPTER TEN

AFTER the holiday, Joanna was hoping that life would settle down into a sort of routine. She was still expected to work extra hours. But Dan never expressed appreciation. He had never even apologised for being unavailable on Christmas night.

She would watch him, using his charm on the receptionists. It was almost possible to be as angry with him as she used to be, at his inconsiderateness towards his colleagues. Several times an angry remark came to her lips. But the charm of that night, the Christmas Eve she had spent in his arms, the unspoken rapture she had experienced at just being close, embraced, treasured—Joanna knew she had been used just as blatantly as the receptionists were used, yet she could not bring herself to condemn him openly.

Malika asked her if she had enjoyed Christmas. 'You got a real kiss!'

And Joanna had to prevaricate. 'What difference is that? He did his duty—maybe it was his way of thanking me for doing a million trillion more hours of work than I'm paid for. I must say I'd rather have the money!'

Malika said, 'You mean that, don't you?'

'Malika, you and I both know that our beloved boss lives in a world of his own. He's fantastic. He's a Greek god. But he's totally outside our real life.

141

Forget it, Malika. OK, I told you I've joined his fan club. But it's not for real. Is that clear?'

'Yes, Joanna.' It wasn't quite clear if Malika believed her, but she had to try.

And Joanna leafed through the medical centre papers on her desk, which made it clear that Melanie Ferrara would be joining their little team at the end of January. That would really be a moment to remember!

Maybe it was the imminent arrival of the lovely dentist that sparked off Joanna's sudden onslaught. Dan was quietly drinking the coffee Malika had brewed for him. Whatever the reason, Joanna had said, her voice threateningly calm, 'You can be a bastard, Dan Bruce. I've never met such a quick-change artist!'

'You have a complaint, Dr Bliss?'

She was looking into his eyes now—the eyes that had been so affectionate, had almost looked as though he needed her. . . Joanna said quietly, 'Not really. The leopard doesn't change his spots.'

'So it's the same complaint.'

'Pass.'

'Joanna, I still employ you. You're under my orders. If you want to alter that, it's in your hands. This might seem like a one-party state, as you so eloquently described it in one of your violent verbal attacks upon me, but no one stays here who doesn't want to. Understand?'

'Yes, Doctor.'

'That almost sounds like insolence.'

'I wouldn't worry, Doctor. You can almost always rely on your sex appeal.'

Dan gave a sudden smile. 'Gosh, thanks, Doctor. I'd almost forgotten my secret weapon!'

'Don't give me that! You never forget how to get your own way, Doctor!'

Dan drew himself up. In a voice that was so neutral that she didn't know if he were teasing her or not, he said, 'I take under my wing a new, inexperienced senior house officer. I train her. I teach her. I go out of my way to give her opportunities to stretch herself, to get new confidence and experience. . .and what happens? She accuses me of laziness! To me, Dr Bliss, that is some insult!'

Joanna faced him. It took courage, because one part of her wanted to compromise, apologise, bring this unseemly and unnecessary debate to an end. She adored working for Dan. She would work for him until her arms dropped off. But she had to remember that once this year was up he would make the same unreasonable demands upon Joanna's successor, unless she made a stand, made it very clear that his behaviour was totally unacceptable. She wanted to say, Oh, Dan, do what you like. I'll go along with it. But instead she said quietly, 'One of these days, Dr Bruce, you're going to get a terrible shock. Let me be the first to warn you. If you go on making use of people as blatantly as you are doing, it will backfire on you, and you'll find yourself without friends, without colleagues. I believe even your devoted receptionists have a breaking point.'

To her surprise, he didn't answer back. 'You mean it, don't you?'

'Yes, I do, Dan.'

'Even though the hotel pays very well? I would

have thought them content to go along with my orders, at such rates?'

He had a point. No one could complain that they were being paid inadequately. Joanna tried to put it another way. 'Many people resent being made use of.'

Dan said, in his sexiest, husky voice, 'What you're saying, Joanna, is that you resent it. No one else does.'

'I'm the one who has to get up and operate on your patients when you aren't available, Dan.'

'You'd thank a consultant in Moreton for giving you the chance!'

Joanna said, unable to find another answer, 'Please, Dan, let's stop this pointless argument. I know I'm right, but you have this ability to put me in the wrong all the time, and I don't want to talk about it any more.'

'You started it.'

'How childish can you get, Doctor?'

Dan smiled, and it melted her. But she had no intention of showing he had any effect whatsoever. He said, 'Argument over, then?'

'Over.'

'I'm so glad. I'm worried that all this aggro will give you lines around your eyes, Joanna!' And in spite of her anger, she had to turn away, hide her smile, so that he wouldn't see how easily he could win her round with a joke and his easy, gentle pleasantness.

And then Melanie Ferrara came to work. She only did two mornings a week, but the first week was quite a strain on all concerned. First of all, the equipment wasn't to her liking. Joanna heard Malika explaining in detail. 'We had the top firm to fit the chair, Doctor. They tore up the floor to make sure you had a foot pedal just where you had told us you wanted it.'

'It's so far out, it might as well be on the beach, woman!'

Joanna tried not to listen. Melanie might have Dan Bruce's affection, but that alone wouldn't make her fit in, if she went on like that. The medical centre had been a tranquil place, apart from Joanna's occasional outbursts at Dan. Now it threatened to become a battlefield.

It was noticeable, too, that Melanie only created a nuisance when Dan wasn't there. That made it twice as difficult to complain about her, because he would make it appear petty. Joanna didn't get involved, but she could see quite well how petulant Melanie Ferrara could be.

Malika was philosophical. 'He understands her. They both come from West Indian families, both born in the Caribbean. I suppose the family background is important.'

Joanna was scathing. 'Good manners don't have a home. It's just as easy to be polite whether you come from the West Indies or Hudson Bay.'

Malika smiled. 'But we have to put up with it, wherever the bad temper comes from.'

'That's true.' Joanna sympathised with the girls, who took the brunt of Melanie's complaints.

'Teething troubles.' Malika tried to make a joke. 'We'll soon understand one another.' Malika did her best. But no one else had much time for the beautiful dentist. She made more fuss about her five patients a morning than Dan and Joanna did for a whole week's work.

When a young woman fell from a horse and damaged her jaw, Joanna had the opportunity of working alongside Melanie Ferrara. Joanna dealt with the physical shock, and admitted the girl on a saline drip. Melanie came along to the hospital, to advise on the procedure, after the front two teeth had been dislodged, and the mouth very bruised. 'I'll set the front teeth back in place. Have you any means of immobilising the mouth?'

Joanna had to admit she didn't know. 'But the girl is in so much pain that I don't think she'll try and eat anything.'

'That's not really good enough, is it, Dr Bliss?'

Joanna was irritated by the other woman's manner. Just because Dan Bruce was besotted didn't mean that Melanie could throw her weight about as though she had some superior position at the medical centre. Joanna said, needled, 'If you have any logical suggestions, please make them, Melanie.'

'Bandaging. Someone will have to bandage the jaw in place.'

'That's no problem.' Joanna smiled to herself, recalling Dan's comment that she spoke the motto like a Hernandean. She had six months left on the island. Could she still say 'No problem', and really believe it?

After a month, Dan came into Joanna's room unexpectedly one morning. 'How do you think we're doing?' he asked her.

'I beg your pardon?'

'You and I versus Melanie Ferrara?'

'I didn't know it was some sort of contest.'

'Does she fit in, Joanna? Or would it be better if she went back to Constanza? And just saw patients when the hotel referred them along to her surgery?'

Joanna said, not wishing to express her own reservations, 'As far as I'm concerned, there were no problems.'

Dan said, with a wave of a hand, 'You've lived in Hernandez too long, Joanna. You've started to ignore problems that matter.'

She looked at him. It was puzzling, that Melanie worked with them, yet Dan still left work on the dot of one o'clock, every afternoon, even the afternoons that she was there. And there was no physical contact. When they happened to meet in the corridor, or in the foyer with the receptionists, there were no hidden glances, no secret touching of hands. In fact, the lovely dentist was given no extra time, and certainly no favours. It began to cross Joanna's mind that perhaps Melanie was not the cause of Dr Bruce's persistent absenteeism.

She wondered whether to tackle him straight out. He was infuriating, yes. Unpredictable, very much so. Exasperating, most of the time. But he had never lied to her. And from past experience he was most approachable when she had given him a real run for his money on the tennis court. The only trouble was, he was always away when she felt like playing. She said so.

'You want a game?' he asked. 'Why didn't you say so?'

'Quite simple. You always go away before I have time to plan my afternoons.'

'Joanna, I have—engagements in the afternoons. I don't deny it. But for you I'd break any engagement.'

She searched his face for any sign of perjury, but it seemed perfectly honest, and quite keen on a game of tennis. She said, 'I thought we could play for money.'

'That's a good idea. What money?'

Her face was straight, as she said simply, 'For all the overtime you owe me.'

Dan's eyes showed that her jibe had gone home. He said, with his voice deceptively calm, 'It doesn't seem to have entered your pretty little head, Dr Bliss, that you're my assistant.'

'I'm very aware of that, Dan.'

'In my book, an assistant shares the work—covers for her boss—fills in when he's too tied up. Are you now telling me that you want extra pay for all the hours that I'm not there? That wasn't in our agreement, Joanna. You're taking advantage of my good nature here.'

She said, 'Shall we discuss that when I win the match?'

His face softened into a smile. 'Suits me.'

'I'll wait for you next Wednesday, then. Three o'clock.'

'You sure it won't be too hot for you at that time? The afternoon sun can be a killer.'

'Not as hot as you'll find me, Dr Bruce, sir. . .'

He called after her, 'Promises!'

Joanna turned back to smile at him. It was hard

to bear a grudge. In fact, she didn't really care about the extra work by now. It was second nature, and she was well aware that the operations she had done and the cases she had seen when on her own had given her a lot of worthwhile knowledge and experience. One day she would tell Dan the truth. But just now it was fun to tease him. And she was agog to find out if Melanie was indeed the shadowy woman, or if they had made a bad mistake, and saddled him with a lover he didn't particularly like, never mind love.

He was on time on Wednesday. In fact he was changed and waiting, sipping a tonic water with one of the coaches. Dan said to the coach, introducing Joanna, 'You know my right-hand man, Pepe?'

Pepe beamed. He was one of Joanna's regular partners, and had trained her up in the past few weeks to what he called 'championship standard'. He said, 'You know that you've got one of my star pupils here?'

Dan pretended to wince. 'Oh, no, man. There's money on this match!'

Joanna said, 'You have a five-minute preparation time, Dan, while I change.'

Pepe called after her, 'You better go easy on this dude, Joanna! He's shaking!'

She left them, wishing that the atmosphere between herself and Dan could always be this easy. She knew she tended to be edgy, whenever he was away without telling her, or when she was left with something she needed advice about. But they had been working together for eight months now. Surely, if he valued her judgement about anything, he ought to have told her where he went on his days off? But no. A brisk wave of the hand, an occasional 'thank you' and he was off, day after day after day. She must be some terrific woman, to command his total obedience like that. Joanna sighed, and wondered what it would be like to be the woman in Dan Bruce's life. To know that he couldn't wait to get home to you. To bask in the full glory of those blue eyes, sincere and loving, concentrated totally on you. What a prospect! What a man!

She changed into her white shirt and short skirt, pulled the laces on her tennis shoes firm, and made an effort to put the romantic image of Dan out of her mind, and concentrate on Dan the opponent. In this field, if in no other, she was almost his equal. And after each match he had always seemed in an expansive, affectionate mood. Praying a silent prayer that the same thing would happen today, Joanna served the first ball.

He had been right. Mid-afternoon was a hot time to play. She won the first set, but weariness prevented her running in the second, and Dan ran away with it, six-two. He called, 'We can leave it now, if you like. The thought of a cold beer is beguiling me away from the courts.'

'Chicken!'

'I'm no chicken, Joanna. But I don't want my favourite assistant collapsing with heatstroke.'

She liked the sound of his name for her. Favourite assistant. . . . She called across the net, 'You mean I'm more of a favourite than our glamorous tooth artist?'

Dan bent double with amusement. 'Oh, Joanna, don't make me laugh. You're jealous of Mellie!'

She hit a ball impulsively at him, but Pepe shouted out, 'Foul stroke! Abuse of ball! Penalty to Señor Bruce.'

That gave him a start in the final set. Dan went on to win in easy style. Joanna hit hard, but she was a woman, and her lesser muscle power told in the end, though her tenacity had her holding on till the very last point. He went to the net and held out his hand. She walked to meet him, took his hand, and said briefly, 'Thank you.'

He said quickly, 'You could have won if you'd waited till evening.'

She said wearily, 'You're never here in the evening.'

'I would be if you wanted me.'

'Liar!'

'Hey, wait. You'd better explain that crack.' But Joanna had walked off the court and along to the changing-room. She didn't expect him to be waiting afterwards, and he wasn't. She walked slowly back to the villa, and shared a jug of lemonade with Rosita before the maid went home. Then she sat in the garden, wishing she hadn't spoken like that to Dan. She liked him so much. It was only his having secrets that she didn't like.

It was still possible that Melanie was his lover. He might have been trying an elaborate cover-up, pretending that she meant nothing to him. But without asking him to his face there was no other way of finding out.

There was a ring at the door, and she ran to

answer it, hoping against hope it was Dan. But it
was Malika, standing with Valentino and Fidel.
'We're going to the baseball match. The boys
thought you'd like to come along,' she said.

'That sounds great.' Malika was wearing jeans, so
Joanna changed into hers, and put on a thin cotton
sweater. She was glad to have the evening filled up,
after her plans for wringing his secrets from Dan had
fallen through. 'Let's go.'

The hotel laid on special buses to Constanza at
night. The atmosphere was carefree and cheerful,
reminding Joanna of her student days. That seemed
a long time ago now. But she wasn't too old and
staid to enjoy the freedom of being with naturally
enthusiastic young people.

They crowded into the floodlit stadium, admiring
and cheering the Constanza heroes, in their white
shirts and padded breeches. There seemed to Joanna
a lot of standing around, of posing and practising
before each ball was struck. But it was great fun,
hearing the partisan crowd cheering their side, and
cheering with them, while the orange sellers, and
the boys with sun-roasted cashew nuts, wandered
around between the aisles, and plastic bottles of rum
were passed along the rows to the regulars.

They wandered along the narrow streets, where
music never stopped, and friendliness and good
humour were the rule. The lights were dim, com-
pared with the hotel complex, where they had their
own generators, and the coloured lights sparkled
day in and day out. But the town bustled with life,
and Fidel explained everything to her as they
walked, from the tailors' shops, still open, where

hand sewing machines turned out frilled and orna-
mented dresses, to the beauty shops, where plump
matrons were having their nails painted.

They ate vegetable pizza at an open-air café, and
then walked back to the hotel, where they danced
for a while with the rich folk. Fidel said, 'I guess
those two want to be alone.'

Joanna looked up. 'I'd better get home, then.'

'You can dance till dawn if you like.'

'Thanks, but not me. Appreciate it, though.'

She was tired. She left Fidel at the dance-floor,
and walked back to the villa through the trees. He
would have no trouble finding partners. She paused
for a moment by the medical centre. It was in
darkness, which was a good sign. Dan was on call,
anyway, and if there had been a call while Joanna
was in town, it was Dan's responsibility. Maybe that
was the only way for him to realise that he was being
selfish.

'Yes, ma'am. Had a good time?'

'Dan!'

'Who else? I am on call, you know. Can I beg a
beer?'

He was standing at her door, leaning on the wall
in the shadows. She smiled at him. Unpredictable.
Infuriating. But so welcome. 'Come in.'

'You don't mind? It's after midnight.'

'I'm not counting. I've had a lovely evening.'

'Dancing?'

'I went to the game. Then for a pizza. Then
dancing. It was fun.'

He said in a detached voice, 'Do you think you'd

like me to renew your contract for another year, Joanna?'

Something in his voice made her cautious. 'Yes, I think so.'

'You're going to have to be a bit more polite to me from now on, then.'

They were in the kitchen, and Joanna had just poured a cold beer into a glass. She pushed open the back door, and they walked idly into the garden. Joanna sat down on the bench, and covered a large yawn with her hand. 'It's been a long day. Thank you for the tennis, Dan. Next time I think I'll beat you.'

'Why didn't you wait for me?'

She looked up at him, surprised at the curtness in his tone. 'I did. But I thought you were angry with me for calling you a liar.'

'I was. But I wanted to clear the air then and there, instead of waiting all night for you.'

'You waited?'

'I waited.'

'Here?'

'More or less.'

Joanna said quietly, 'You're sometimes more than flesh and blood can take, Dan Bruce. Do you realise that? I asked you to play tennis for the simple reason that on the last two occasions we've had a civilised conversation afterwards.'

He laughed shortly. 'Conversation? You don't go out with Fidel Carrero if you want conversation!'

'I didn't know anything about his reputation. He was very gentlemanly to me.'

'I'm relieved to hear it.'

'I'm glad you're relieved. It makes it easier to say goodnight, doesn't it?'

Dan turned away, drained his glass, and put it down on the bench. 'If that's what you want.'

'No, I'd like to talk—even though you are in a bad mood. It's better to talk it out than keep it to yourself. Are you telling me that I may not get another year's contract with you?'

'It's up to Riaz in the end. But I have a say.'

Joanna was puzzled by his persistent bad mood. He had often teased her like this, and ended up with a laugh. Tonight his voice was grim, and there was no sign of the happy ending. She said, 'If I've offended you, I'm very sorry.'

'I don't believe you. You've never been able to accept me as the boss, have you? Always wanting to know where I was, unwilling to take your share of the work.'

She said unhappily, 'Not always. I'm used to it now.'

'Or was it this you wanted?' He didn't seem to hear her reply. Instead he caught her roughly in his arms and kissed her fiercely, taking her mouth and using it with his, making her gasp for air. 'Am I as good as Fidel, Joanna? Do I measure up to the latest boyfriend?'

CHAPTER ELEVEN

IT WASN'T easy, trying to pretend things were normal, when Joanna went in to work next morning. But she had to try. It would make it even harder to work as partners, now that she had really quarrelled with Dan—a serious quarrel, not one of their regular little snaps, which served to clear the air and keep things easy and natural between them.

But Malika noticed something. She came into Joanna's room between patients. 'Something really bad has happened to Dr Bruce. I've never seen him so bad-tempered—and absent-minded. He isn't concentrating on his patients at all.'

Joanna felt guilty. 'I hope it isn't my fault. I know we tease each other a lot—I thought it was part of our relationship. But I may have gone too far. I may have said something that really hurt him. I wish I knew.'

'Don't blame yourself. We all know how difficult he can be to work with. You've been a heroine, the way you've stood up to him.'

'I'll have a word with him later,' said Joanna. 'Apologise, if it's my fault.' But she had little hope. Their bitter words to each other the previous night still rankled. And that kiss. As though he was trying to hurt her physically as well as verbally. She had never been kissed like that, and his lack of tenderness hurt her more than the pain of his lips.

Malika noticed. 'Have you hurt your mouth?'

'No.' The reply came out rather too quickly.

Malika said, 'Better put some lipstick on, Joanna.'

After she had gone, Joanna took a close look at herself in her handbag mirror. There was a bruise above and below her lips. It wasn't very noticeable, but Malika had spotted it. Joanna found a compact, and tried to powder the marks away.

To make matters worse, Melanie Ferrara came in late, and complained loudly to Malika about the lack of proper instruments. Malika had to tell the new dental nurse where everything was, while Melanie huffed and puffed and said what a waste of time it all was.

'We don't want her anyway,' Malika muttered to Joanna as she took away the notes of the patients that had been seen. 'She disrupts the nice atmosphere we used to have. I don't know what's happening today.'

'I'd better go along and see if I can calm things down.' Joanna started with Melanie. The pretty dentist was dressed in silk trousers under her white coat, and, even wearing metal-rimmed glasses, she still looked like a fashion model. Now that she was beginning to know where everything was kept, her temper had cooled, and she greeted Joanna quite warmly.

'No, nothing wrong now, thanks. Once I get used to the place.' She had a little girl in the chair, and Joanna was impressed by Melanie's gentle tone, and the way she chatted to her patient, putting her quite at ease. Joanna left, hoping against hope that having

Melanie close by would act in a soothing manner, and raise the gloom of her impossible boss.

Dan next. She tapped on his door.

'Come in,' he called. 'Oh, it's you, Joanna.'

He was sitting behind his desk, composed and businesslike. He didn't stand when she went in, but then he hardly ever did. She said quickly, 'Send me away if I'm interfering, Dan. But if there's something wrong and it's my fault, I want to know how I can put things right.'

'Malika has said something?'

'I think all the staff sense that things aren't right.'

He said ironically, 'You were anxious to needle me last night.'

'You know as well as I do, Dan, that we've sparred like that many times, and you've taken it in fun.'

He nodded, and stood up, walked over to the window. 'Could be. It's my fault, then.'

'I thought so last night. You were so rude about Fidel Carrero, and there was no reason to say anything.' He turned to look at her then, and her indignation vanished at the sight of the sadness in his eyes. She said, 'I'm sorry, Dan. I'm really sorry. I don't know what's troubling you, but I hate to see you like this.'

His eyes hadn't moved from her face. He didn't speak for a moment. Then he put out his hand and lightly touched the bruise on her upper lip. She winced away from his hand, and he swung on his heel and looked out of the window again, his hands clenched at his sides. 'A bit of a brute, aren't I?'

'No. No, you're not. It was probably what I said.'

'Don't make excuses for me.'

'Dan, is there anything I can do?'

'Yes, there is. Can you take over and let me get away early?'

'Now?' It was only halfway through the morning. But she shrugged her shoulders. She had asked for it. If he wanted to get away to the arms of his loved one, then perhaps it was the best thing to do. He obviously needed some comfort, and he clearly wasn't getting it here. 'Sure. You go ahead,' she told him. But the pain and frustration of not being able to give him what he needed made her voice shake. There was nothing in the world she wanted so much as to be able to bring back the teasing light to his eyes, and the lilt to his voice.

And then there were voices, agitated and alarmed. Malika came running in. 'Doctor, a boy has been run down by a car. They're bringing him in. Shall I call Dr Jamis?'

'Yes, please.' Dan sprang into life. 'Bring him in here. Joanna, will you check the waiting patients as soon as possible? If they can come back tomorrow, then ask them to. Otherwise, tell them you'll see them this afternoon.'

'OK. I'll get on to that right away.'

Dan looked across, suddenly directly into her eyes. 'Thanks, Joanna.' And she felt the impact of his blazing sincerity, and knew she would never meet a man she could love and admire so much, however long she lived, or however ill-mannered he could be at times.

She went to the waiting area. This would require much tact. There were seven patients waiting,

soothed by the taped music, and by the beauty of
the fountain. Joanna said, 'I'm Dr Bliss. We have an
emergency road accident just now. I'll be happy to
see you at once, if you have an urgent problem.
Otherwise, I can come along to your rooms this
afternoon, if you leave your names with our
receptionist.'

They came, one by one, and told her their problems, and Joanna decided it was quicker to see to
them at once in her consulting-room. She heard the
frantic coming and going outside the door, as the
accident victim was taken through to the hospital.
She was doing the right thing by seeing the minor
patients. But she knew how much Dan wanted to
get away from the medical centre, and was anxious
for him to have the chance.

The patients had been seen, and she was standing
at her desk, putting the last papers away. Then Dan
came in. 'Come with me, Joanna? I need you.'

'I'm just coming.'

He said, already turning away, 'You've never let
me down, Joanna. Not once. There ought to be
some kind of award.'

'There is.'

'What?'

'I'll tell you some day.'

For a moment their eyes met, then he turned. 'It's
internal—I think the boy has a ruptured spleen.'

'Let's go, then.'

He said, 'If I have to leave, could you manage by
yourself?'

She said quietly, 'Yes.'

'OK, let's go.'

She followed him. Memories of his humour, his teasing, the times when he had accused her of liking him—knowing very well that she found his style of management unorthodox and unacceptable—where had all the happiness gone? He was more or less expecting her to remove a damaged spleen for him. How far could her loyalty go? She looked at his proud figure as he walked in front of her to the operating theatre. 'I'm doing this for myself, you know,' she said.

'I know, Joanna.' He didn't look back. 'Sense of duty and all that—I understand. You couldn't do it for a man who was crazy enough to bruise your—feelings.' He meant mouth, but couldn't say it. She felt compassion, though she knew she had a right to be distressed.

They started the operation. Joanna knew she could cope. But dragging a spleen from its moorings—even when all the arteries had been tied—was a tough assignment, and she was relieved that Dan did the hard work before leaving her to suture.

He was long gone when she changed from her theatre gear, and made her way back to the foyer. She explained to Malika what had been done. 'It was a tough operation. The patient is young—he'll be OK in an hour or two. We've left instructions with the ward sister.'

Malika said, 'Dr Bruce asked me to tell you he had to go. He said he was sorry to leave you in charge.' She smiled, a little wanly. 'He never thought of apologising before. Why?'

Joanna smiled back. 'Our chief is exactly what you told me when I was new here: a law unto himself. I was unhappy until I recognised that as the truth. But now—I don't know, Malika. I've got used to his bad manners. I'm worried about him.'

'We all are.'

'There isn't anything that I can do.'

'You don't know where he goes, when he leaves here?'

Joanna said, 'I've never asked outright.'

'Maybe if you followed him. . .?'

'Wouldn't that be wrong?'

Malika said, shaking her head, 'It would be wrong if I did it. But you, Joanna—you have a closer relationship with him now. Anyone can see that. He trusts you.'

'I'm not so sure.'

'I am.'

Joanna refused Malika's invitation to go for a swim. Her mind was troubled. In all her turbulent months working as Dan Bruce's sidekick, she had never felt that she was wasting her time. She had thrown herself into the work with increasing enthusiasm. And now, suddenly, the time for reapplying for another year loomed. And she desperately wanted to stay on. Since breaking with Roger, there was little to lure her back to her grey British Midlands. She had found colour, excitement, challenge. And she had found Dan Bruce. If only she had some explanation of the sudden change in their relationship!

'Dr Bliss—what on earth are you doing looking so glum? I've had so many messages of thanks from guests who appreciated what you did for them.'

Joanna looked up from her simple cheese and

pineapple lunch. 'Hello, Señor Riaz! Sorry not to notice you. I was thinking.'

'I hope it was about coming back next year.'

'Yes, it was, actually.'

'Dr Bruce has submitted no other names,' he told her. 'It would make my schedules tidier if I could write you in as a definite.'

Joanna looked up into the cheerful, podgy face of the general manager of the Palacio. 'If it only needs my signature, Señor Riaz, you can have it now. But I feel we ought to consult Dr Bruce.'

'Well, yes, naturally. But I believe his approval can be taken for granted. He has given me glowing accounts of you.'

Joanna said nothing. Naturally a man who wanted time off would give glowing accounts of someone who was sufficiently under his thumb to deputise whenever he wanted. 'OK, then. Put me down as definite,' she said. But while Señor Riaz went off, content that at least one position for the following year was settled, Joanna felt a lot less certain that Dan would approve.

She was so locked up in her own thoughts that she didn't realise someone had taken the seat opposite to her. When he leaned across the table and put his hand on hers, she shook herself from her reverie. 'Oh—it's you, Fidel!'

She looked around for Valentino. Fidel said, 'I'm alone, Juana.'

She wrenched her thoughts back to the present moment. 'Sorry. A few things to sort out in my mind.'

Fidel Carrero leaned over and looked into her

eyes with a smile. He was very good-looking. His smile was even and honest, and his dark eyes promised paradise. And now she knew he had a reputation as a Casanova. 'Sort them out soon, *princesa*! Hernandez isn't the place for thinkin'. It's a place for enjoyin'.'

'With you, no doubt,' she smiled.

'Sure with me. Who else?'

'You know, I'm flattered, Fidel. You such a young man, and me such an old professional doctor. . .'

'You are one of the loveliest women I've met, Juana. . .' he pronounced it the Spanish way '. . .and I'm willin' to hang around with you just as long as you say so.'

She leaned across and met his gaze with a broad smile. 'Thanks, Fidel. You've given my pride a big boost. But there's someone in my life, and there isn't any room for anyone else.'

'So?'

'So go and find someone available, man!'

'Is he as good-lookin' as me?'

'Could be.'

'Is he around?'

'Well, no.'

'How long you gonna wait?'

'Forever.'

Fidel stood up, recognising defeat. 'Sugar, I hate seein' a beautiful woman wastin' herself.' He leaned over and kissed her cheek very lightly. 'See you, *princesa*.' He took a step or two away. 'If you change your mind, we could make music. You look as if you know how!'

She said without looking back at him, 'And I'm right out of tune.'

Next morning, Dan was at his desk before Joanna got to work. But there was no recrimination, no joking, not even a reference to the fact that she was a few minutes late. Joanna said to Malika, 'If he asks, I didn't sleep last night.'

Malika nodded. 'I think I could tell, Joanna.'

'I look that bad, huh?'

'A bit peaky. But the bruises have faded.'

Joanna shook her hair back, suddenly embarrassed. 'I'll start, Malika. Send the first patient in.'

Between patients, Joanna pondered. The way things were just now, they couldn't get any worse. The idea that had been at the back of her mind started getting more insistent. Follow him. Find out just what it is that's causing him so much pain. If he found her following him, it wouldn't make things any worse than they were now. She could commandeer a jeep at the flick of a finger. Joanna commandeered.

The driver clearly wanted some action. 'You don't need me? *Señorita*, you don't know what terrible roads we have! You need me! It's going to rain—bad!'

'I know the mountains, Carlos. I've done it!' She didn't say she had done it in ideal conditions. Why bother? She had made up her mind to follow Dan Bruce, and following Dan Bruce was a tactful operation, not needing the services of anyone else. 'Thanks, anyway.'

She edged back into the medical centre. Surely no

one had noticed her stealthy absence. She was self-consciously chatting to Malika when Dan came out of his room. 'I'm off, then, Malika,' he said. He didn't see Joanna.

'Yes, Doctor.'

'Dr Bliss OK?'

Joanna said quietly, 'Of course. Don't worry, Dr Bruce.'

Dan turned. His eyes registered preoccupation. 'I have to get away,' he explained.

'Sure. No problem.'

For a split second he saw the joke. But the curtain came down over his face before he had time to acknowledge that he recognised her use of the Hernandean motto. In an instant they could all hear his Ford backing out of the car park. And before anyone had time to look back, Joanna had slipped out of the side door, started up the jeep, and was waiting, the engine idling, until she saw the nose of Dan's Ford edge out of the main avenue, and take the highway towards the mountains.

She drove a way back, giving Dan no inkling that he was being followed. It had been a while since she had driven, particularly in a right-hand-drive car. But the need to know where Dan was heading made her forget the handicaps. She followed him through the town, only getting nervous when he took the mountain road. She knew where the car lights were. But she had arrived over this mountain pass, and she knew just how hazardous it could be, particularly at corners.

It was still early afternoon. There was no need to fear the onset of dark yet. Joanna drove slowly, keeping track of Dan as he steered the long Ford upwards, towards the uplands. She began to recognise the landmarks. There were billowing clouds in the blue sky today, but they didn't look threatening.

The road wound upwards. The little jeep handled better than the car she had hired when she had driven here just a few short months ago. That day when she had stopped on the other side of the mountain to ask the way, of a tall blue-eyed Greek god with a naked torso and powerful muscles, who leaned on a native scythe to look at her in scorn. . .

Inside the forest, it grew very dark. At first Joanna was glad of the shade, but then she realised that above the trees the clouds had come down, and covered the mountain in mist. She began to feel cold—and apprehensive. Yet there was only one road, and she couldn't get lost if she stuck close to the edge and just waited for the road to start going down again.

The rain began to come down. Fortunately the cover of the jeep was up, but it didn't appear to be very watertight. She was feeling very guilty now for even thinking of trailing Dan, realising it was none of her business. But it was too late. She emerged from the trees on the other side of the mountain, and came thankfully out of the cloud, damp but unscathed.

There was no sign of Dan's car by this time. Joanna felt bad—she had decided to turn round as soon as she could, and take the road back. She had made sure that Dr Jamis was available if there were any calls from the hospital. All the same, she knew she had no right to be here.

Then, suddenly, she recognised the grassy bank where she had first met Dan Bruce. It was still raining, and the track was muddy and slippery. But at least she knew where she was, and there was a narrow path that led off the road towards a group of small huts. It was her only chance to turn. Joanna took it, and turned left into the small settlement. Beyond the huts there was a stone building, and she realised it was a convent. Two nuns sheltered under a rough tarpaulin, while one of them reached up to cut two coconuts from a leaning tree.

They looked up as Joanna turned in and stopped. One of them came towards her. 'Good afternoon, traveller. Are you lost?'

A voice answered for her. 'No, Sister. She's looking for me, I think.' Dan came forward, his shirt soaked, careless of the rain. 'You'd better get inside, Joanna.'

She was made welcome inside the cool stone convent, and provided with a cup of hot coffee. Then the nuns left them alone. Joanna said, 'I shouldn't have done it. It was a stupid impulse.'

'As you're here, you'd better see what you came for.'

'What's that?'

'My girlfriend? Isn't that what you suspect?' His voice was neutral, and it made her feel ashamed. 'She's this way.' He led her along a dark corridor into a tiny room, where four beds were arranged against the wall, their sides pulled up like children's cots. Dan led the way to the furthest cot. 'This is my mother, Joanna. She doesn't know me—hasn't known me for a long time. And now she has pneumonia. No, don't look shocked. It will be a blessing if God takes her at last.'

Joanna looked at the peaceful face, the white hair, the little shape hardly making a hump under the well-worn cotton coverlet. 'Oh Dan, why didn't you tell me?'

He shrugged. 'She wouldn't have wanted it. She was a very proud little lady, very jolly. We used to have such good times.'

Joanna looked out of the window. The little village shacks were neatly arranged, with small patches of vegetables and pineapples, and trees bearing bananas and papayas. 'This is what you do,' she said. 'Work in the Sisters' garden.'

'It's the least I can do. They've been angels to Mother.' He looked back at the sleeping figure. 'After Father died, I brought her with me from Jamaica. You can see that it would have been unsuitable for a fashionable resort like the Palacio to have an old lady spoiling their image.' He didn't sound bitter, only practical. 'So I consented for her to be kept here, with the proviso that I was free to see her every day, once we employed a suitable deputy.'

'I see.' Joanna felt humble. 'I was wrong to jump to conclusions.'

'To think I kept a mistress out here? It's understandable, I suppose. I did seem very keen to get out here, I know. I have a feeling it was Malika or Juanita who probably put the idea of another woman in your mind first.'

Joanna said humbly, 'Thank you for telling me. I promise to say nothing to anyone else.'

'I think maybe I was wrong to keep it to myself. I see now that colleagues who work with me have had a lot to put up with. The least I could do was put them in the picture.'

'Maybe, Dan. But I'll say nothing unless you do. I'll just go back now, and say I turned round when the mist came down.'

His troubled expression lifted a fraction. 'You must have been scared.' His blue eyes almost twinkled. 'Serves you right!'

'I'll go back. I'll just thank the Sister for the coffee.'

'Don't be foolish, Joanna. The rain's coming down. The road will be very slippery. You can't go alone.'

'The jeep is reliable.'

'But you aren't, woman! You don't know these mountains. Wait just an hour, and I'll drive you back. We can come back for the jeep another day.'

'Very well.' She sat quietly, while Dan went out to chat to the villagers. She looked through the window, saw him stroll from hut to hut, sometimes taking out his stethoscope to listen to a baby's chest, look at a sore limb or feel a child's neck for lymph nodes. This was his other life, caring for the poor people who couldn't afford to go to a hospital. He took out tablets and medicine from his black bag and gave it free. He dressed an old man's ulcerated leg, and gave a crying baby an injection of penicillin for its earache, which soon stopped the pitiful wailing.

Then he came back to the convent. 'We can get back now, Joanna,' he said. She followed him, feeling very ashamed.

CHAPTER TWELVE

JOANNA said, on the way back, as Dan negotiated the slippery track with nonchalant ease, 'I'd like to help, if you'll have me. With the village, I mean. It's a long way for you to come almost every day.'

'I don't mind it. It's second nature now.'

'Well, if there's ever a day you don't feel like going—the offer stands.'

'You think I'd let you loose on this road? I seem to remember—wasn't it you who stopped and asked me if you were on the right road to Constanza?'

'Yes.' So she hadn't made an impression on him. Unlike her vivid remembrance of him and his rudeness. 'Naturally you wouldn't recall these things—being worried about your mother.'

'Oh, I remembered you, all right. Foolhardy, even then.'

Impertinent, even now. Joanna said nothing. Having seen him in the pouring rain looking after the villagers, she felt she had no right to speak back to him. Yet he was the same Dan, who had teased her and joked with her. It was a pity that those carefree days were over. The mental picture of his mother would always come between them now.

And there was the question of next year. Joanna had made it clear to Señor Riaz that she wanted the job. But it was very unlikely that Dan would want her around. She had invaded his privacy, without permission and without welcome. She, single-handed, had ruined their relationship. She sat quietly in the car, and said no more. She had a fatalistic feeling that at the end of the year Dan would be quite content to say goodbye.

Next morning Joanna met Malika at the café for breakfast, quite by chance. She was fully prepared for questioning, but to her surprise, Malika didn't mention Dan. 'Valentino said he loved me last night.' She smiled happily.

'Well, good for you. Did he mean it?' Joanna quietly buttered her croissant, and hoped they could keep the conversation to Malika's love-life.

'He once told me he'd never say it, because there were so many beautiful women in the world and he didn't want to deprive them of the pleasure of falling in love with him.'

Joanna laughed aloud. 'I can imagine Valentino saying that!'

'You don't think it's because he wants a more sexual relationship, do you, Joanna?'

Joanna nodded. 'Probably. But it's better to stand out against that sort of guy. He'll respect you because you're different from all the others.'

'But if I stand out against him and then lose him to someone else?'

Joanna said carefully, 'I'm no expert, Malika. But maybe losing someone who only says he loves you on that basis might turn out to be a blessing in the end.'

'That makes sense, Joanna. But I'm getting on, you know—I'll be twenty next birthday. I feel I ought to be settling down.' Malika didn't even notice Joanna's protest at her being so young!

They walked to the medical centre together. Malika remembered, suddenly. 'You were going to follow Dr Bruce!'

'The weather beat me.'

'Oh yes—it did rain yesterday. Will you try again?'

'No.'

'You don't want to know?'

'No. We have no right to pry. He's in charge here—he'll tell us if he thinks we ought to know.'

'You're quite right. I felt bad about suggesting it really.'

Joanna went to her consulting-room, her guilt making her quiet. Oh, for the days when she could shout her head off at Dan, and get as spirited a reply back! Those days were gone. And soon her very days at the Palacio would be numbered. No more beach parties, no more juicy pineapples for lunch, vigorous tennis matches under the strip lights, no more moonlit dances, and chicken *a la criolla*. And no more stolen kisses from Dan Bruce either. . . She remembered the first one. The excitement because it was illicit, when she was still an engaged woman, yet she couldn't stop herself responding.

After work, she walked along to the foyer to chat to Malika. 'Coming swimming?' asked Malika.

'Yes, why not?' She couldn't tell Malika how much she dreaded being told that there was no job here for her next year. Yet she couldn't bring herself to beg. Dan knew she wanted the job. She dared not try and force him to decide.

They walked to the beach, and ate their usual fruit salad. Malika ran out for a swim, but Joanna felt lethargic, and lay on her sun-lounger, pretending to sleep. She heard footsteps nearby, but didn't bother opening her eyes until she heard Dan's voice. 'Tired, Joanna?'

She sat up. 'You didn't go to——?'

'No. I'll go tomorrow. It's painful, watching her, knowing there's nothing I can do.' He squatted on the sand beside her. 'I thought I'd come down and see what you two get up to every afternoon.'

'Very little, actually.'

He smiled. 'You've enjoyed your year, then?'

'You know I have.'

'You'll have a lot more experience after this— should be a great plus when you apply for a general practice traineeship.'

'Oh, yes. Terrific.' Joanna couldn't put any enthusiasm in her voice.

Malika came running up the beach, dripping wet. 'Oh, Dr Bruce—shall I get you a sun-lounger?'

'No, thanks, Malika. I just thought I owed you girls an explanation.'

'What about, Doctor?'

'About my mystery trips. You see, Malika, Joanna—my mother is still alive. She's very old and very ill—and she's being cared for at a convent at the village of Santa Barbara in the mountains.'

'Gosh!' Malika was staring.

Dan said with a smile, 'You thought it was a woman, didn't you, Malika? You were right.'

'Oh, Doctor——!'

'I don't blame you. But I realise I should have

told you two—you've been very loyal, and I should have trusted you with the truth. I'm sorry.'

Joanna said in a low voice, 'We're sorry. We knew you must be under some kind of pressure. . . I hope she—has an easy end, Doctor.'

'I think she will. She's in no pain. I'll go and see her again tomorrow. Meanwhile, Joanna, I feel like hitting a tennis ball very hard. Will you join me later?'

She felt honoured—surprised. Why her? 'I'd like to.'

'I'll book court twelve if I can. I always win there.'

'You always win everywhere.' And Joanna didn't only mean at tennis.

Dan stood up, and looked down into her eyes. 'At four, then?' He left them.

Malika stared after him. 'Poor man! We've teased him so much—and thought bad things about him. I know I resented him going off so much—I thought he was enjoying himself!'

'So did I.' Joanna sighed audibly, thinking of the patient way he went from house to house, treating the poor barefoot villagers as respectfully as he treated the rich hotel guests at the Palacio. That was what being a real doctor was all about. She said, almost to herself, 'I always liked Dr Bruce. Now it's so much more. . .'

She lay back, her eyes closed, but her mind racing. It was nice of him to invite her for tennis. In a way he was saying that they could still be friends. But by following him that afternoon she felt she had forfeited his trust. They could never be as close as they had been. Just friends. Just good friends. And she would go back to England, and after a while the bright, colourful people of Hernandez would become just a distant memory. A tear slid from under her eyelid. 'No problem,' she whispered to herself. 'No problem.' But it was.

Dan was waiting at the court when she showed up in her tennis whites. He smiled, and flung her a couple of balls. 'Be gentle with me, Joanna!'

With a trace of her old fire, she called back, 'No quarter! If I give you an inch, I'm finished.'

'Am I really such a brute?'

'I think it's called being a good player. Having the will to win.'

'Well,' he called back, 'if something is worth having, it's worth fighting for.'

'I'll remember that.' She hit the ball, running round the court with new energy. Dan might have been talking about tennis, but Joanna was thinking about her job. It was worth having. So she was going to have to fight for it to keep it. Dan Bruce would find she would take him at his word.

As usual, she took a set off him, but he won the final set by making her run until she was weary. They walked back along the alleyway between the courts, out of breath and quiet. At the pavilion he said, 'I'll wait for you.'

'All right.' She felt nervous. Peace seemed to have broken out between them, but it felt like a fragile peace, that the slightest careless word would break. How could she fight for her job, when she was nervous at what his reaction might be?

He was indeed waiting for her. His pale hair was brushed neatly, and he wore a tailored shirt and trousers. Joanna's heart turned over at the sight of those blue eyes, at the smile on his lips when he saw her. He said, 'How about coming for a drink?'

'Sure. I'll leave my things at the villa.'

'May I leave mine too?'

'Of course. Rosita will make sure they're laundered for you.' He followed her into the house, and she suggested that he mix the Cuba *libres* the way he liked them. They took their drinks out into the garden, where the sun's rays were almost horizontal as it started to set in familiar glory behind the casuarina trees. Everything was peaceful and beautiful.

Dan said softly, 'I'm glad we cleared the air, Joanna. It was time I told you and Malika about Mother. I didn't realise how secretive I seemed to you. I just got into the habit of telling no one. But then I'd never been as close to anyone as I was to you.'

'I—I'm glad you say so. I thought we were almost friends. But then I felt so guilty at—spying on you. Yes, that's what it was, Dan—no fancy words, please. And I knew after that you wouldn't feel the same about me.'

He said casually, 'It did make a difference, I must say.'

'I knew it would.'

'For a start, I realised how much you cared about me—about what happened to me, and about why I was so depressed the other day. It's a new feeling, having someone care.'

She said gently, trying not to be too impertinent, 'How about the million beautiful women?'

'Oh, yes, those women.' He smiled as he stared out over the garden in the dusk. The fireflies danced, and beyond the garden the fairy lights went on in the distant trees, making the grounds of the hotel a permanent Christmas.

Joanna said, 'Dan, you said it was right to fight for what you want?'

'So it is.'

'I want my job.'

'I know.'

'How do I fight for it?'

'Just keep doing it properly, and I'll keep your name at the top of the list.'

'You have a list?'

'Oh, yes.'

'Señor Riaz said there were no other candidates.'

'How long ago did he say that?'

'A few days.' She said, 'You have no complaints about my work?'

'Not at the moment.'

'Is there any way I can do it any better?'

Dan laughed suddenly. 'Oh, Joanna, you're sweet as sugar, you know that?'

'But that isn't a qualification for assistant medical officer.'

He took her glass from her hand, and set them both down. Then he took both her hands in his. 'I've got the message, Joanna. You don't need to fight any more tonight, OK?'

'All right. But I won't stand by and let you appoint anyone who doesn't work as conscientiously as I do. Or who expects more money and more time off. I'm not asking for any rise at all. Exactly the same contract will suit me, you know.'

He said quietly, 'It looks as though there's only one way to shut you up after all.' And he bent and took her lips with his. For a moment they stood, still holding hands. Then his arms went round her, and they clung together, kissing with a gentle sensuality, taking and giving pleasure.

Joanna heard the pager going off in her shoulder-bag indoors, and for a moment thought she was imagining it. Then the insistent bleep sounded again, and she took her arms from Dan's neck with great reluctance. 'I have to go,' she sighed.

'I'll come along.'

'All right.' They hurried across the gardens together, forgetting they had just played a strenuous game of tennis, as well as going through emotional depths that it was hard to tear themselves out of immediately. Joanna's irregular breathing was due as much to the closeness of Dan's hard body as to the sudden dash to the hospital. Juanita was on duty. 'What is it, Juanita?' Joanna asked her.

'A young girl. Her mother is very alarmed—she says she is talking nonsense. And she is very pale, Doctor.'

Joanna was reaching for her stethoscope the moment she entered the consulting-room. The pale, rather slim girl of about fifteen sat on the edge of the couch talking to her mother. 'Will I die, Mummy? Will Daddy die? I should be at school, you know. Miss Andrews will be cross. There's nothing wrong with me.'

Her pretty black eyes were wide, the pupils large.

Joanna said gently, 'Lie back against the pillow, dear. What's your name?'

'Philippa Ward. Who are you? Are you from the school?'

'I'm the doctor. Can I listen to your heart, Philippa?' It was slow. She took the blood-pressure, with the sphyg Dan had already taken out of its case. 'The pressure is low, Dan.'

'She seems hot to me.'

Joanna took out her thermometer. The mother said, 'She was hot when I first noticed her talking gibberish. But then she became very cold, and started shivering.'

'Has she had anything like this before?'

'Nothing. But she's been complaining of feeling very tired for the past couple of months. I just thought she was growing too quickly, and needed feeding well and getting lots of sleep. That's why I brought her away on holiday. I thought it was just what she needed, to get away from the pressure of school work when she wasn't feeling one hundred per cent.'

'Nothing wrong with that, señora. If you have no objection, I'd like to admit her to the hospital ward for some blood tests and overnight observation.'

'You think it might be something serious, Doctor?'

'Not at present. But I think she may be anaemic. We'll keep an eye on her until we get the results of the full blood count. You can stay with her if you like.'

'Thank you very much, Doctor. I was so relieved when they said there was a doctor on call. When I saw the medical centre in darkness I was very worried. You've all been very kind.'

Joanna rang for the nurse. 'Make Philippa comfortable and arrange for a cup of coffee for her mother,' she instructed. 'And I want to be called if there's any change in her condition whatsoever.'

She stood with Dan after the girl had been taken to the ward. Dan shook the blood he had taken from the girl's arm, in its small phial, and gave it to a lab assistant to be analysed. 'It's a mystery to me,' he said. 'Delirium like that usually comes with a high temperature, but hers was just below normal. Swinging, though. Up and down, her mother said.'

Joanna nodded. 'It might be a viral infection. I'll go along and have a quiet chat. She may have some mental problems she hasn't told her mother.'

'Worry at school, or boyfriend trouble. Could be, Joanna—but my bet is simple anaemia causing bizarre symptoms. A couple of iron injections may be very painful at first—but the improvement is quite dramatic.'

'I hope it's as simple as that. Thanks for your help, Dan. I'll go along and have a private chat, woman to woman.'

'Good luck.'

She smiled up at him. Colleagues, they were now, Friends and colleagues. If only the patients knew how the two doctors had been passing the evening before the pager sounded! Dan smiled back, and as he passed her on his way to the door, he bent and kissed her forehead very lightly. As Joanna hurried along the corridor, she touched the place he had kissed, and wondered if it meant anything. Did he want her as an assistant next year? It looked like it just now. But Dan was still an unknown quantity—unpredictable as ever. She knew she would have to wait until he was ready, before she knew for certain if she had the job.

She sat and tried to talk to Philippa, but the girl seemed very sleepy all of a sudden. That would fit the diagnosis of anaemia. 'You aren't worried about anything you haven't told your mother?' Joanna asked her.

'Only that I might die. Mummy would be upset if I died—and if Daddy died too. He has a tumour, you know. He might die.'

Joanna went to the mother. 'You can go in now. Have you let your husband know about this?'

'My husband has been dead for three years, Doctor.'

'Tumour?'

'No. He had a heart attack. Philippa was away at school. I think she felt sorry she didn't see him before he died.'

'Yes—I think maybe she still does.' Joanna went back to her room, unsure about whether to spend the night in the hospital. The girl's problem seemed more mental than physical. There seemed little she could do until they got the blood test results.

When she woke, she was still in her chair, her neck felt stiff, and the morning sun was streaming in through the slats of the blinds. 'Oh, bother! Now I'll have a stiff neck all day, and I haven't time for a shower.' She splashed water on her face and neck, cleaned her teeth and tried to smooth out her crumpled dress.

The duty nurse looked in. 'Doctor—you never went home! Would you like some breakfast?'

'Good idea, Josefina. Thanks.' After buttered toast and hot bitter Hernandean coffee, Joanna felt brighter. 'First things first. Have they got any results from the lab for me?' But they were still working on the sample. Joanna walked round the hospital and checked the three in-patients. She had almost forgotten just how luxurious the rooms were, how well equipped, and how polite the staff. The thought of going back to the Moreton way of medicine, the making do, the endless shortage of beds, instruments, and equipment depressed her. She sighed deeply. If only I could stay just one more year.

The lab technician popped his head in. 'Doctor, I haven't finished testing, but the haemoglobin is OK. Just half a degree down.'

'Thanks for letting me know.' Joanna walked back to the ward. If the girl wasn't anaemic, there had to be some other explanation of her symptoms. 'Philippa, have you had your breakfast?' she asked. Her mother wasn't in the room—a golden opportunity to get to the bottom of her problems. Joanna sat on the bed. 'You get on well with your mother?'

'Sure.'

'And you go away to school?'

'Yes.' Hesitancy. Joanna thought immediately that school might be getting on top of the girl. Exams were one of the main worries of kids of this age. Joanna asked a few more general questions about school. Academic achievement didn't seem to be a difficulty. Then Philippa said, 'But there's a good school near my home. Mum seems bent on spending too much when I'd do just as well in my home town.'

It tied in. The poor girl was away when her father died. It made sense to want to be at home more. Gently, Joanna elicited the truth. Yes, Philippa had never wanted to leave home. Her parents had thought they were doing the right thing. And now her mother kept reminding her how lucky she was to have a sixth-form place at the prestigious boarding school. Joanna said bluntly, 'You'd like to stay at home?'

'I would, Doctor.'

'Have you ever thought of asking your mother?'

'I couldn't do that. It would sound very ungrateful.'

'Shall I do it for you?'

'If you think——'

'You won't get better in this depressed state, my dear. I do think it's the best thing for you.'

'So do I, Doctor.'

Joanna talked a little more with the girl, and saw her face brighten, the more they talked about the school near her home. 'Leave it to me, Philippa,' she said.

At that moment Philippa's mother returned. 'I'm sorry, Doctor—I only went out for a shower. If I'd known you were coming——'

Joanna sat her down, and talked gently about her daughter's happiness. 'You can see that sending your child away could be looked upon as rejection?'

'Surely not! The best school in the county?'

Joanna explained. 'She was there when her father died. She had a great sense of insecurity, that something is going to happen to you. I'd advise you to inform the school right away that she won't be going back. Otherwise, we have an almighty psychological problem. Do you see what I'm driving at?'

It had taken almost all morning to sort out this little family. Joanna prescribed a short course of iron tablets—but she knew she had tackled the main problem at its source, and that young Philippa would get the security she craved. She went back to her room with a warm sense of achievement, and pressed the intercom. 'I'm here, Malika. Any patients for me?'

'Dr Bruce has seen them all, Doctor.'

'Oh, dear. He won't be too pleased!' Joanna joked with Malika. 'I'd better make myself scarce. I need a decent bath and a sleep, after falling asleep over Philippa's problems!'

'Better still, would you mind stepping into my office, Joanna?' It was Dan, standing quietly at the door.

'Of course.' He was angry, no doubt, after having to do the entire workload this morning on his own. She stepped past him, and walked along the shadowy corridor to his consulting-room. He followed her, and closed the door after himself.

'Would you sit at the desk, Joanna?'

She looked at him uncertainly. Sit behind his desk? 'You're the boss.' She sat down.

'In front of you is a contract.' His voice was very low. 'Joanna, I'd be pleased, proud and very honoured if you would agree to work with me next year.'

She looked up, a broad smile on her face. 'You

really mean it!' She looked down at the contract. 'If you can lend me a pen, I'll sign it right away before you change your mind.' And he handed his pen over with a smile, as she scribbled her name without even opening the contract and reading the second and third pages. 'Was there really a list, Dan?'

'There wasn't a list. But even if there were, you'd be head and shoulders above any other applicant.' He sat on the edge of the desk and looked down at her. 'I was watching you handle that mother and daughter, Joanna. If there were a medal for tact, common sense and damned good medicine, I'd be happy to recommend you.'

She looked up into his sky-blue eyes, touched by their open sincerity. 'Thanks, Dan. Hearing you say it definitely means something.'

He pointed at the contract. 'Would you mind signing the last page?'

She looked down. 'Sure. Sorry, I thought you only needed one signature.'

'No, two.' She turned the pages. Behind the main contract, which was stapled together, was a hand-printed sheet of plain paper. She read it through, looked up at Dan, then read it through again. It read, 'I, Joanna Bliss, hereby promise to marry Daniel Christopher Bruce as soon as possible.'

Her heart was exploding with joy and excitement, but she kept her voice steady. 'You want me to sign this?'

'Yes, please.'

She took the top off the fountain pen and wrote her name, a little less steadily than the last time.

Without looking up, she said, 'Well, I suppose it's different from going down on one knee.'

Dan took the paper and waved it to dry the ink. She looked up into his wonderful face, with its beloved eyes and untidy mane of hair. He really did love her. He really was hers, all hers. The expression in his face said so. He said softly, 'I'll do that too, if you like?'

'Oh, no, Dan, don't! Don't ever become conventional. It's so much more fun just the way you are.' She watched him look at the paper, and fold it in four.

He put the paper in his inside pocket. 'So no problem, Doctor?'

'No problem, Doctor.' Joanna looked into his eyes.

He was kissing her very thoroughly when Malika put her head round the door. She closed it again, with a broad smile, without either of the doctors hearing a thing.

An Irresistible Offer from Mills & Boon

Here's an offer from Mills & Boon to become a regular reader of Medical Romances. To welcome you, we'd like you to have four books, a cuddly teddy and a special MYSTERY GIFT, all absolutely free and without obligation.

Then, every month you could look forward to receiving 4 more **brand new** Medical Romances for £1.45 each, delivered direct to your door, post and packing free. Plus our newsletter featuring author news, competitions, special offers, and lots more.

This invitation comes with no strings attached. You can cancel or suspend your subscription at any time, and still keep your free books and gifts.

Its so easy. Send no money now. Simply fill in the coupon below and post it at once to -

**Mills & Boon Reader Service, FREEPOST,
PO Box 236, Croydon, Surrey CR9 9EL**

NO STAMP REQUIRED

- -

YES! Please rush me my 4 Free Medical Romances and 2 Free Gifts! Please also reserve me a Reader Service Subscription. If I decide to subscribe, I can look forward to receiving 4 brand new Medical Romances every month for just £5.80, delivered direct to my door. Post and packing is free, and there's a free Mills & Boon Newsletter. If I choose not to subscribe I shall write to you within 10 days - I can keep the books and gifts whatever I decide. I can cancel or suspend my subscription at any time. I am over 18.

EP03D

Name (Mr/Mrs/Ms) _____

Address _____

_____

_____ Postcode _____

Signature _____